Stories

Of

Lost

Souls

Any resemblance to any person living or dead or to any location mentioned in the text of any story is purely coincidental.

Copyright: Peter F Damsberg

The Sorting Office	5
The Admiral Benbow	19
Planetarium	29
Pier Island	39
Class Reunion	49
The Dowager's House	59
The Mansio	71
Captured On Film	81
The Man on the Bench	89
Taken Into Care	103
Tunnel Vision	111
The Zookeeper	121
Zig-Zag Street	131
Random Acts	137

The Sorting Office

It was a bright, clear, cool day. The sky was blue, pale with a slight haze towards the horizon, and a deep cloudless blue high above. The old multi-storey building reached out and up into it, a finger, or more a thick thumb, silhouetted in grey against the blue.

From where he stood a single face of the building was turned to his. A regular pattern of dark squares showed where the, on each floor, there had once been windows now bricked up. Except, that is, for the ground floor where the windows had been filled in with breeze blocks which someone had gone through the expense of painting the same light grey of the building. On this side he could see a single large door.

The whole edifice stood alone in a square of disused ground still scattered with the remnants of whatever had occupied it in the past.

He had arrived early. He always liked to arrive early for meetings. He could never be late. He would always plan for the journey carefully and leave in more time, too much time said his colleagues, to arrive at his destination.

He breathed in the air and could almost taste the coolness, but the expected freshness of it was masked by what was the over present taint of brick and concrete dust that still hung over the sire after who knows how many years,. But he was used to it; he was used to building sites. In fact he took some pleasure in the smell. Building and construction was his life and the smell represented the possibilities that existed in this world, the possibilities of turning derelict land, or even open fields, into something more useful - new buildings.

He liked the smell of the open field sites, but when the bricks arrived and the concrete was poured he did not miss it.

And then there was the profit that accrued from his work. Although, if it was just profit that motivated him he wasn't sure that he would enjoy his job so much, it was the act of constructing something new, something to be used, something useful, replacing what was redundant, it was what gave him pleasure.

He looked at his watch. He still wore one; many people did but no longer looked at them much, unlike him. They had their smart phones, but so did he. They were on them so much of the time, so often; their watches were now becoming redundant much like the land he stood upon. Times change. Out with the old, in with the new.

There was still another ten minutes before the agent was due. He did the same as the others, he took out his phone, he checked his messages and emails and, in order of precedence, replied to the one's that required little attention the others he flagged for later

He put his phone in his coat pocket and followed that with his hands to keep them warm. A moment later he heard the crunching of footsteps coming towards him from behind. They neared and slowed.

"Good morning. Mr Vane? I hope I'm on time?" said a voice.

Mr Vane looked at his watch as he turned. The agent was precisely on time, to the second. He was impressed.

"Yes," he answered, "and you must be Mr Guy of Guy and Partners?"

"I am." Said Mr Guy holding out his hand to be shaken.

Mr Vane took his right hand from his warm pocket to shake it. Mr Vane's hand was cold, almost icy cold, and it was thin with long fingers. But his grasp was surprisingly strong. He wore a sharp blue-black suit, a crisp white shirt and a red tie. He had a red silk handkerchief in his breast pocket. His hair was black and wavy with a hint of grey on the sides. His hair wasn't short, nor tool long, but because of the waves he could get away with it growing longer than someone with straight hair and it not looking untidy. His eyes were as sharp as his suit and the same blue-black colour. Small lines, crow's feet Mr Vane thought they were called, were drawn to the side of each eye. When he opened his mouth a single gold tooth sparkled in the sunlight. He was clean shaven, his cheeks and chin shiny and smooth, almost too smooth. Mr Vane wondered if any hair grew at all on his face. It was difficult to judge Mr Guy's age

"Pleased to meet you." Said Mr Vane with a nod and turned to face the building again.

"So this is the building?" he asked unnecessarily, and felt unease at the question being so needless.

"Yes, it used to be owned by the Post Office, a sorting office I believe, before they moved it out of town near the motorway. As you see it's right next to the railway station. They used to unload the mail trains and take the mail over a bridge to it. The bridge has gone now."

Mr Vane smiled inwardly that Mr Guy had made the same error by stating the obvious.

"And the whole building and surrounds are up for redevelopment?"

"The whole thing. It has full planning permission as you would have seen, everything's approved. What with finances as they are these days they'd like to get a deal as quickly as possible, but it has taken time to get anyone to finalise. All previous parties have backed out at the last minute. There's still not enough confidence in the market." Mr Guy paused. "Are you confident?"

"If I wasn't I wouldn't be here. Shall we ..."

"Yes, why not, let's have a close look at it." Agreed My Guy.

They walked towards the building and the dark oblong of the door. They crunched across the rubble. It had been covered by and early morning frost but the sunlight had been warm enough to melt any of it that the rays had touched. In the shadows of the debris the faint white of the frost remained. And in the sharply outlined shadow of the building the frost still glistened and made the shadow less of a shadow; it was more an outline in grey of the building, itself grey.

Various attempts at graffiti covered parts of the walls. Nothing like the works that covered some of the city's buildings, and certainly not like some of those painted by the famous artist. It seemed to Mr Vane that these were just squiggles of coloured paints, looking like people's initials, monikers he believed they were called.

They stopped at the door. It was a large solid steel door a shade darker grey than the building.

Mr Guy pulled out a bunch of large keys from his coat pocket. His coat was also grey as were his trousers. Mr Vane thought that Mr Guy blended in remarkably well with the building.

My Guy inserted one of the large keys into the door. He needed the strength of his hand to turn it. He took the key out and returned it to his pocket. He pulled on the door's single raised handle and pulled. It was heavy but it swung open quietly.

Mr Vane stood back allowing Mr Guy to enter first.

It was dark inside, very dark, black in fact.

Mr Guy had stopped by the doorway and My Vane had come a couple of paces further in and could see nothing.

There was a solid clunk and strip-lights flickered on and off. Mr Guy had pulled a large switch next to the door. The lights went off and on. Slowly they settled down and were all alight giving out a bland yellow-white glow.

"Thank goodness for that." said Mr Vane.

"There would be no point coming in otherwise."

They were in an entrance lobby of some sort. Ahead of them there was a wide opening in the wall that led to another room.

Mr Vane walked forward to it. The lighter dust on the floor rose in the breath of air of his passing and slowly settled back onto the heavier sediment. His shoes, heavy ones with steel toecaps which he wore for site visits, left the pattern of their soles as he walked; one step at a time.

Mr Guy followed him.

Mr Vane walked through the opening. He came into the room beyond. It was large. He imagined, from a mental calculation, that it might encompass much of the footprint of the building. The strip-lights were arranged in identical rows spaced evenly apart.

He breathed in. The air was surprisingly dry and unmusty. He had expected it to be otherwise, most closed derelict buildings he'd entered always had been. He felt there should have been the decay that damp air brought with it. But here the sealing of the building had kept it out and there was just an odour free dry dereliction to it.

Perhaps, thought Mr Vane, it was like that when the archaeologists first opened up the great pyramid; the dry desert air trapped inside for what had been expected to be an eternity but had eventually been breached.

Mr Guy came up beside him.

Mr Vane looked around the inside of the large room. The structure was basically sound. It might look like it needed to be demolished but there was still the possibility that it could be converted to new offices or even apartments. But would the cost be worth it? And how would the structure fit in to an overall scheme for the site? It was much more likely that it would need to be demolished after all, a mix of new buildings of glass and steel erected throughout the site; offices, shops, restaurants and cafes, and new apartments for young professionals. The only one fly in the ointment as far as new apartments were concerned was the law concerning affordable homes. They would have to provide a percentage of them in the mix; that is, unless they could prove it to be unprofitable, in which case they could get away without providing any.

It was right next to the railway station. The city was now becoming popular as a commute for as far as London, it would appeal to the commuters as well as the locals. It would be interesting if they could reinstate the bridge across the tracks offering direct access to the station, another plus point. If that was the case he must make a note to include a hotel in the plans.

Mr Vane didn't have to think much more about it, demolition was the answer.

"So, what do you think?" asked Mr Guy.

"I think it is as I expected. I read the prospectus and the more detailed reports we were given and I don't think I've changed my mind at all. The board was convinced that there is a respectable return on the investment, but it will certainly entail demolishing this building. I don't think it fits in with our plans." Mr Vane told him.

"Oh." said My Guy. "I'd always hoped it could be refurbished somehow. It's a bit of an iconic building to some people."

Mr Vane shrugged. "Just the usual sixties brutalism; I have to admit there are some architects that still view them with some admiration, but not me. And I think most ordinary people would agree with that. Of course I'm no architect, more of a figures man."

"Still," said Mr Guy, "it would have pleased some."

Mr Vane said no more, he couldn't understand why anyone would want to keep such bland concrete eyesores when they could have new, gleaming, clean structures; out with the old, in with the new.

My Vane walked a few steps forward taking a final look at the walls and ceiling. His shoes scuffed through the dust and detritus strewn across the floor. His eyes looked down from the ceiling and walls to the floor. He scanned the debris on it.

Amongst the dust were what looked like pieces of paper. He moved forward another couple of steps to where they were less covered. He bent down. He brushed aside some of the debris.

Yes, there were pieces of paper on the floor. He gave them another brush of his hand. He could see now that they were envelopes. His had reached to one and picked it up. He stood and cleared the final film of dust from it. There was a name written on it.

He bent down again and picked up a few more. He cleaned the film off these as well. Each had a different name written on it, each clearly in a different hand.

They must have been left here from when it was a sorting office and ended up scattered across the floor.

But why? Why were they not sorted, why hadn't they been delivered?

It was obvious. Each envelope had a name upon it, but no address. They could not be delivered.

Still, it was bad form to have left them here.

He suddenly had a feeling that the building should not be demolished without someone picking up and saving the envelopes; that they should not be left here, that the building should not be brought down on top of them and then taken away to be dumped into some landfill or crushed on site to make aggregate for the new buildings.

He had been looking around, inspecting the envelopes and thinking for several minutes. Mr Guy had been standing behind him but had said nothing not had he been heard to move.

Mr Vane turned to speak to My Guy.

He was not there.

Mr Vane had not heard him go, he must have returned to leave the building after they had spoken thinking there was no need to stay. Mr Vane now agreed with that sentiment and headed back to the entrance lobby and the outside door.

He walked into the entrance lobby and towards the door.

He stopped. He looked.

There was a wall, but there was no door; at least no door where he had expected one or where there should have been one.

He walked closer to the wall. It was a solid grey wall. There was definitely no door nor had there ever been one.

He must have gone through the wrong entrance and come into a different lobby. He walked back to the main room. He looked at each of the room's walls. There was no other entrance or exit.

He began to get a feeling of foreboding, of not understanding. It was impossible of course, there had been a way in, a door, and they had used it, he and Mr Guy.

Mr Guy, he would be outside, and he knew that Mr Vane was inside.

All he had to do was contact Mr Guy. He had the phone number, and he had his phone in his pocket.

He reached for it with his left hand. In his right hand he still had the envelopes and dropped them back onto the floor. He took the phone from his pocket. He turned it on, looked for Mr Guy's number and pressed to dial it.

The screen flashed up a message. It did not connect. He looked at the bars on the phone; there was power, plenty of it, but no signal. He tried again. He was faced with the same result. He tried his office. It was no good, there was definitely no signal, he could call no-one.

He stared at the phone's screen. His mouth became dry. He must keep calm. He had always been able to keep in any situation, and he must do the same now. There was an explanation for this, there had to be; a simple explanation, something obvious that he'd missed. He would retrace his steps. It must have been his mind playing tricks on him last time he had looked for the door.

But his mind had not been playing tricks on him. The reality was still the same. There was no door. No way out. No escape.

It wasn't now just a feeling of not understanding, it was knowing that he did not understand that turned his foreboding into something more fearful. He felt his heart rate rise and beads of sweat appeared on his brow.

There had to be a reason for what was happening, something rational. He had to think it through, figure it out. He must work through, in his mind, every moment leading up to this, his predicament. He thought and he thought. He went over every second since he had come to this place. But what had happened still made no sense. Logic dictated that what had happened could not have done. But it had.

He now had his phone in his right hand. He looked at it again. There was still no indication of a signal. He went to put it into his coat pocket. He stopped short. There was something in his pocket. He was sure it hadn't been there before. It was an envelope. It must be one of those he had picked up earlier. But he thought he had dropped them all not put one in his pocket.

He put his phone in his pocket and pulled out the envelope. The obverse was facing him He turned it. There was a name written on it, written in black biro. He always used a black biro himself.

The name was his.

His name was written on the envelope in black biro.

But he had not written it. He knew he had not written it. He would have remembered writing it. But it was his name on the envelope in his hand.

It must be some trick. That Mr Guy had somehow placed it in his pocket without him noticing. This whole thing was some sort of trick, some sort of sick joke, maybe some way to pressure him to agree to paying a higher price for the development.

He opened the envelope. It was empty. It was nothing but an envelope. He threw it down on the floor. It landed on top of the others he had thrown down, facing upwards, his name in black and white. His and the other names, some in black others in blue, in what must be biro or in old fashioned pen and ink, stared up at him from the floor.

Enough was enough. He ran back to the lobby. He stood before the wall where the door had been. He shouted. He cried for help. He screamed out Mr Guy's name as loudly as he could. He did so again and again with as much force as he was able.

He banged on the wall with his fists. He banged until his hands hurt, until the rough concrete of the wall caused them to bleed. He shouted until his throat became hoarse.

He stopped. He had lost control. He did not lose control, but he had.

He stared silently at the wall which stood in its own silence before him. No sound came from beyond the wall, from outside the building, all was silent.

He still didn't understand. He needed to understand.

He stood before the wall. His breathing had been heavy but now he calmed himself and his breathing slowed. He stared at the wall. It was blank and his mind felt the same.

The light changed. It briefly went a little darker, for less than a second, just a flicker of darkness.

He turned. He looked at the opening and the sorting office beyond.

Again a flicker of darkness, then light.

He stared. He had a bad feeling in his stomach.

Another flicker, two, three. Patterns of darkness spattered around the sorting office, briefly at first, then more of them and for longer.

The lights were failing.

Where was the switch? It had been on the wall next to the door. He looked. There was no switch.

Flicker. Flicker, flicker. Flicker, flicker, flicker.

And then the flicker of lights above him, not in the sorting office but in the lobby.

The lights were going out and he would be left in the dark.

One by one the strip-lights died.

He just stared and waited. What could he do? He could think of nothing.

Flicker.

The last of them, the one nearest to him, went out.

He was alone and it was dark, very dark, black.

He stood. He could not think. He could not from a thought yet alone be able to work out what to do. He just stared into the blackness. He might have screamed but he was all out of screams, and if he had it would have been swallowed up by the blackness, sucked into nothingness.

He had no idea what to do.

He usually had ideas. He usually knew what to do.

Now he knew nothing; had nothing. It was only his breathing that gave away his existence.

How long he stood there he wasn't sure. But something, time perhaps, brought his mind back to life.

He had his phone, didn't he? It had a battery, it had power, and it had a torch. He had light.

He took it out. He checked it for a signal. Still none.

He looked at the time. He must have been inside for about two hours but it had seemed much shorter.

He pointed the light towards the sorting office. There must be a way out. There could not be just one entrance or exit. Surely there should be doors to other rooms, stairs to the upper levels.

He stared walking towards the sorting office.

His torchlight flickered.

He stopped.

It flickered again.

The battery had been over 80%, it could not be failing already. He looked. It was. Something had drained it.

For a moment he froze; what should he do now? If it failed now he would be caught in the middle of the lobby, caught, trapped in emptiness. He couldn't bear that thought. Should he go forward to the entrance to the sorting office and that wall or go back?

He turned his phone off to try and conserve some power and returned to the outside wall. He stood with his back to it. It was something solid to feel, something firm to hold onto.

What was possible, even in the blackness, was to follow the wall around the lobby and into the sorting office, then follow and feel those walls around to try and find a doorway. One that would lead him out of here or maybe upstairs.

He would do it calmly and carefully, taking his time, not panicking and keeping his breathing steady. He began to feel his way around the lobby.

He had only got to the first corner of the lobby when he halted. Something had changed. Things were not as black as they had been, in terms of light if not in his situation.

Looking towards the opening from the lobby to the sorting office he did not expect to be able to make it out, but he could. There was a very faint glow coming from inside the sorting office outlining the entrance, a square block of very pale light against the black surround. One of the strip-lights must be working, partly if not fully. He left the wall and walked to the entrance.

He peered into the gloom.

The light was not coming from the ceiling. It was not coming from one of the strip-lights. It seemed to be coming from the wall at the opposite side of the sorting office, from the wall itself. The wall had a light blue glow to it, brighter towards the centre. Maybe it was where a door would be.

He hesitated trying to decide what to do. Should he go forward? He supposed he must, what else was there for him to do?

As he was about to move the glow increased. He stayed where he was, at the entrance to the lobby, and put a hand out to hold on to the wall. It gave him some comfort.

The glow grew in one particular area. It became brighter. At the centre of the all at floor level the glow began to take shape. It was an oblong. It was the size and shape of a door.

As he took a step forward the light in the shape of the door coalesced, the outline of it hardened, and the rest of the wall dimmed. What remained was a white door. He hesitated again, wanting to go forward but wary. Then a sound came from the door. He listened and looked. It was the sound of a key in a lock, turning. He stayed still. The sound came from it, he knew it had. And then, slowly, the door opened inward. Beyond it was darkness, but that of night-time not of entombment.

It opened fully and a figure appeared in the doorway.

A man stepped into the room. He was on the short side and he wore a uniform.

His coat was blue with red cuffs and a collar trimmed in gold. He wore grey trousers and a red waistcoat with brass buttons with a watch chain hanging across it. On his head, making seem taller than he was, he wore a tall blue hat with a wide brim and a gold band around the base. Over his shoulder he carried a leather bag on long straps.

The man closed the door behind him.

My Vane wanted to shout, call out to the man, cry for help, ask him to get him out of there. But he didn't. There was a paralysis in both his body and his voice.

Mr Vane knew that what he looked at was a door, but knew it wasn't a door; it could not be a door. Doors do not appear out of walls as if my magic. For that matter, they should not disappear either.

But he needed a way out of here, he had to get out. And it was the only door.

The light from it lit up the room in an eerie blue glow.

The man had not, apparently, noticed him and moved forward keeping his eyes on the floor. He came towards the half way point and stopped. He tutted and shook his head.

Mr Vane could not stand silently by any longer. He cleared his throat and managed to speak.

"Excuse me." Said Mr Vane, his voice breaching the air.

The man started, looked up towards Mr Vane and took a step backwards. His eyes were wide. He said nothing but clutched his leather bag tightly to him.

"Excuse me." Said Mr Vane again. "I need help."

For a few seconds there was silence. The man looked at Mr Vane and Mr Vane looked at the man. Mr Vane was about to repeat himself when the man spoke, in a higher pitched voice than Mr Vane had expected.

"They all want help Sir."

"I need to get out of here." Mr Vane explained. "I'm trapped; I can't find any other door."

The man shook his head. "I don't know of any other door, Sir. Just the one. And I'm the only one with the key as far as I know."

"Then you can let me out of here."

"Once I've sorted everything Sir, yes, I could let you use the door. But everything has to be sorted first. Just look at it all," he said pointing to the floor, "nothing sorted everything in a mess."

"What if I helped you." Said Mr Vane, thinking that any speeding up of what this man wanted to do would mean a quicker release.

"Oh, no Sir. You have no authority. I do the sorting."

"Very well. I'll let you get on with it. The quicker it's all sorted, the sooner I'll be out of here."

The man looked at him, considering. "Very well Sir."

The man turned to the floor, bent down, and began picking up the envelopes, brushing the dust away and carefully reading each one before placing them in his bag. Mr Vane watched him. One by one he picked them up, brushed them, read them, and put them in his bag.

Mr Vane had to ask a question. "I suppose you are someone from the post office. How can they be delivered, there are no addresses on them?"

The man looked up at him with a bemused expression. "Names Sir, they have their names on them, who else could they for except the person they are for?"

"Yes," said Mr Vane, "but how do you know where they are if there are no addresses?"

Mr Vane thought he would ask but he had heard that the post office had a special department to deliver mail that was incorrectly addressed, and very good they were at it too if the TV reports were anything to go by.

The man was answering him. "They have their names Sir, in their own hand, there is only one place they can be. They cannot be in more than one place now, can they? They can only be where they are, where else?"

My Vane sort of understood what he meant; but not really.

"There," said the man, picking up an envelope, "the last one."

The man read it. There was a look of mild surprise on his face.

"I believe this one is yours Sir."

Mr Vane didn't understand for a second or two and then remembered.

"Ah, yes, that must be mine. I found it in my pocket. I must have dropped it on the floor."

Mr Vane walked forward towards the man with his hand outstretched to take the envelope from him. But the man whisked it away and put the envelope in his bag.

"Oh, no Sir! I'm sorry Sir, it's been collected now Sir. It must be delivered to the correct place. I'd be in trouble otherwise, Sir."

"But I'm here in front of you! Why don't you just give it to me? Not that there's anything in it anyway, it's just an empty envelope."

"Oh no Sir! More than my job's worth Sir. And I'm not to know what's inside. That's very much against the rules."

"But there's nothing in it."

"There's always something inside Sir. That's what envelopes are for. Why else would anyone send them Sir?"

"But it's been opened. I opened it. There's nothing inside."

"You opened it Sir!" the man gasped, horrified. "You opened an envelope here in the sorting office, before it had been collected and delivered?"

"But it's my letter, with my name on it, written in my hand, therefore my property. I had a right to." Said an exasperated Mr Vane.

"Not in here Sir, not in the sorting office, before it's been delivered."

The man turned and moved towards the door, Mr Vane a step behind him.

""I'll go with you, you said I could."

"That was before I knew what you done Sir." Muttered the man.

"But you've got to let me out, you can't leave me here!"

The man was using the key to open the door.

"I'm not sure it will let you Sir."

"What do you mean 'let me'; just open the door and let me through, that's all."

The door was open. The man turned around to face Mr Vane. He put his hand in his bag and pulled out an envelope.

"Here Sir. You may as well have this. I know I shouldn't, but well ..."

Mr Vane took it. He didn't want it. He'd no reason to keep it. He let it fall to the floor.

The man had stepped through the door. It was closing. Mr Vane took his step to go through before it shut.

He was half-way through.

The wall lit up, the whole wall. There was no oblong of a door, there was just the wall.

Mr Vane wasn't sure what happened. One moment he was in a doorway, the next he was not; all there was, was an eternal grey.

The wall was solid. It had returned to its grey colour, a grey colour in the blackness of the room.

And Mr Vane with it.

A letter lay on the floor, dust gradually accumulating upon it.

-:-

FOR SALE

Large site for redevelopment. Existing offices suitable for refurbishment with large area of cleared ground ready for new construction. Planning permission granted for residential and commercial properties.

Available immediately.

Guy and Partners, Bristol

The Admiral Benbow

It was the time of the year when, in the stillness of chill air, leaves floated one by one from the trees lining the cobbled street along the docks and gradually built up in the gutters and on the sides of the paths. Those that fell upon the narrow road were slowly ground down by the traffic and mulched by the lying film of water and finally taken away by heavier cold rain or drizzle. It was the time of year when the days were changing from those of long hours of light to longer hours of darkness.

Aiden worked in an office that faced the cobbled street and the old quays and docks. It was an old building. The frontage, however, had been upgraded over the many years – several centuries – that it had occupied its place there. Once inside many of the offices had also been improved so much so that it would have been difficult to differentiate them from any others in the city; bright lights, computers, and modern office furniture were the ubiquitous style. The one exception was the board room. Its walls were panelled in ancient oak, oil paintings of long gone directors hung around the walls and the boardroom table and chairs looked as old as the panelling.

The Company had been formed several hundred years or more earlier. Aiden had never been told the actual date. It had been set up by a group of Merchant Venturers. The money they made from their more obvious investments in tobacco, sugar and, yes, slaves, needed a vehicle for safer, longer term investments; and so the Company had been formed. Its name, Woodes, Crispe and Colston, was unknown to many who lived in the city but not unknown to those of the city. It kept a low profile. It handled investments for private clients but also took an interest, both academically and financially, in new, up and coming, business and proposals. They were by no means stuffy; they were well informed as to the latest advances in technology and commerce and canny enough to see future potential in new ideas and investments.

Aiden had been recruited a year earlier and had spent much of the time to date integrating with the people, procedures and modus of the Company. The Company did not rush such things. He had now been given his first assignment; a young entrepreneur with what looked like an intriguing we-based proposal. The young man had raised funds trough family and friends but now needed more substantial investment to move forward. It had seemed just the thing for a young man such as Aiden to cut his teeth on, and he would no doubt be able to interact well with someone his own age.

Aiden had met his client, Justin, twice before. They had gone through the business plan together. Aiden had managed to ask the right questions and uncover some inconsistencies that needed answers and suggested some further background and support work that would hold the proposal together more firmly. They had got on well.

Earlier in the day Justin had called Aiden and suggested they meet up after work. The city was not Justin's home and for the time being he was living in a bed and breakfast. He had been a student at one of the city's universities, had loved living there, and intended to make it his new home. It was also the sort of place, entrepreneurial with just the right mix of small up and coming web based businesses that made it an ideal place for the start up.

But living in a bed and breakfast had its draw back's and Justin was keen to avoid the four walls of his room. On the early evening he would go to a gym, one very close to Justin's office on the old quayside. He had suggested to Aiden that they meet up for a drink and maybe something to eat after he had finished there. Aiden had agreed. It was a Monday evening and he had nothing else planned. And being a Monday it was possible to have a quiet drink unlike the weekends. Monday was always the quietest night of the week for the food and drink industry; Aiden knew that, he had seen the graphs.

It was just before 7pm when Aiden left the office. Only a security guard and two cleaners were left in the building. He didn't have far to walk, the gym was only a matter of yards down the street. The street itself was quiet, workers had gone home and people were yet to come out for the night. The odd car would take a short cut through this backstreet rumbling over the cobbles as it went, and a solitary cyclist or two would make the best of it over the uneven ground. The streets lamps lit up the cobbles in a way that they didn't on flat tarmac; they reproduced the rippling effect of the waters of the docks.

Along the dockside, passed the gym, there was a line of boats that had been converted into bars and restaurants. On the landward side it was the same, old buildings once used as warehouses now converted into offices and upmarket restaurants and bars, or their glass replacements of similar chain hotels, although amongst them there were that had been converted into student accommodation which had livened up the nightlife.

Aiden reached the gym at seven. He waited outside for a few minutes and then Justin emerged. He carried a sports bag over his shoulder and was wearing jeans and a blue Nike top. Aiden was still in his suit.

They shook hands and Justin suggested they go along the dockside and turn off into a side street that had a good selection of pubs, bars, small clubs and restaurants. This street too had once been an important part of the docks. A street that had always had its fair share of bars and inns which in the days of sailing ships would have been rowdy and sometimes dangerous places, where a man may have been press-ganged into the Navy.

Several of the pubs still existed. Indeed they had been preserved and could not be altered.

One pub in particular was connected with old tales of pirates and other mariner's tales being the supposed inn belonging to Long John Silver, The Admiral Benbow of Treasure Island fame. Here too was where Daniel Defoe was aid to have met Alexander Selkirk the original Robinson Crusoe, and had got the idea for the novel.

It was the closest of the pubs as they turned the corner into the street and the one Justin suggested they went into. Above the entrance hung the unusual pub sign – 'The Llandoger Trow'.

The pub was large and, of course, old, which meant that it was something of a labyrinth of smaller rooms rather than the wide open spaces much loved and created by the pub company designers. In the centre of the pub, after passing through an area which might have once been two rooms, there was a single bar. On the counter were menus.

"What would you like to drink?" Justin asked Aiden.

Aiden had been here before and knew the selection of beers and ales well enough but, since his student days he had been drinking cider, it had been cheaper than many beers and lagers and the habit remained. He asked for a pint of the local Somerset brew. Justin chose a Guinness; extra cold.

"How about something to eat?" Justin asked as he perused the menus.

They were much like those in any pub chain. Even though this was a very individual place it was still owned by one of the major pub companies. The menu hardly needed any looking at to know what was on it.

"Or, maybe," said Justin, "we could have a drink here and go for a Chinese or Indian. There's two really good one's just down the road.

They had waited a while to get served. There was only one barman, in fact only one person working, and it looked as if he was both barman and cook. Not that the place was busy. There was only one other, elderly, couple sat at a table just finishing a meal and small glasses of white wine. Justin and

Aiden took table that was almost hidden form the couple and unseen by the barman.

They chatted about the business plan and the changes Justin had made to it and then moved from the subject and on to the usual topics of football and women.

Aiden heard the sound of a door and looked to see the elderly couple leaving. No-one else had come in and they were now the only customers.

They'd finished their first pints and Aiden went to the bar for refills. Once again it took some time to get served. Aiden had to knock on the counter a couple of times with a coin to attract the hidden barman's attention before he appeared from beyond another room. There was no apology and the barman served him without a word, just a couple of nods and grunts. Obviously, Aiden thought, the man was English; any foreigner would have a better attitude to work

He took the drinks back to the table.

As they sat and begun their drinks the lights flickered and dimmed. They flickered once or twice more, by which time the barman had brought out some candles in small glass lanterns, placed some on the bar and lit them. Then he began going from table to table doing the same. His final candle was brought to their table and he lit it.

"Expecting a power cut?" Aiden asked him.

The man grunted. "Always a problem. This place don't like electrics."

As he said it the final glow of the electric lights vanished leaving the pub in candle light.

"There you go." Said the barman. "Back to the dark ages."

And he walked back to his hideaway.

"Oh well," said Justin, "makes it feel like a real old fashioned pub not just an imitation."

"With a real old fashioned barman." Added Aiden.

Justin smiled. "True, you don't see many like him about these days. From what my granddad's told me all the old pub landlords used to be miserable old so-and-so's, just like him."

"Perhaps his granddad trained him." Suggested Aiden.

"I wonder if he's got a certificate for it? Five stars for apathy and poor service. They could design a notice to put up outside the pub like the ones for hygiene."

They both laughed.

"Could actually be quite an attraction." Aiden said. "Now, there's a new business idea for you! People might come from miles around just for the experience."

"Organised trips from abroad even!" suggested Justin.

"Except from France." Said Aiden seriously. "They'd always beat us hands down for contemptuous service and disdainful waiters."

"True." Nodded Justin. "True."

The door opened. Aiden had changed his position slightly since getting back from the bar and had a better view of it. A single man walked in. Around him blew in a cloud of mist. Outside the door it had been very dark. No light came through it, nor did any come through the windows.

"Looks like the street lights are out as well." Aiden told Justin. "And a fog's come in off the water. Looks pretty grim out there."

"Perhaps we may as well have ordered something to eat here?" Justin suggested.

"Let's finish these and see how things are. Maybe the lights will be back on by then. If not we can have another here."

The man who had walked in was at the bar. There was no sign of the barman. His frame stood out against the light of the candles. Aiden thought that he looked rather strange. He wore a long coat almost down to his ankles and it was probably black, but everything in the shadow of the candlelight looked black, and he wore a hat. Looking at it in silhouette it looked like a small chimney on top of a roof.

The mist from outside still seemed to flow around the man but Aiden realised that it must be smoke, surely not a cigarette, it must be an electronic one. They were allowed in pubs but seemed to give off more vapour than tobacco smoke would have done. You could get them in all sorts of flavours, even, he supposed, tobacco.

And that's what Aiden could smell. More like an old fashioned pipe than a cigarette though, and a smell he didn't find too unpleasant, in fact as it wafted over he found himself liking it.

"Is that man smoking at the bar?" asked Justin with a frown.

"I think it's just a vapour one that smells like tobacco."

"Smells like the real thing to me."

The man turned and looked at them.

Both of them quickly looked away and carried on talking. They didn't want him thinking that they were staring at him, though of course they were.

They both heard him. They heard the rustling of his coat and his footsteps coming across the floorboards; steady, solid, confident footsteps. Neither of them wanted to look.

"Well, now, me hearties." The man said in a slow, unusual and grating West Country accent.

They looked up at him.

His face was weathered. It was tanned, lined and leathery, but clean shaven. His eyes were blue-black and piercing but had a tinge of being bloodshot around the edges. The hair that fell from under his hat was black, long and had waves to it. He had a gold earring in his left ear. He smiled. His lips opened and he showed off a single large gold tooth.

In his hand he held a pipe. It was electronic one, it was a pipe, a real one; and it was old, it had a long stem and blue smoke curled up from the bowl.

"Let me purchase you a drink young Sirs." said the man, leaning forward and placing his hands on the table.

Aiden and Justin recoiled slightly. They could smell the smoke and a sweet smell of some exotic tobacco on him. There was more to his scent than that; a smell of the sea and of tar and other odours which, to the young men, were unfamiliar.

Aiden spoke. "No mate, thanks, we've still got half a pint left. Thanks all the same."

The man stood upright. "Mate is it? You have a fine sense of precognition young Sir, to know I was a mate. But I must insist. I must purchase drinks for you. A glass half full is half empty, and in my world needs filling."

Before they could speak the man had turned and headed to the bar.

"Why is there always one weirdo in any bar?" asked Aiden.

"And he was smoking. Did you see that? Why didn't the barman stop him or tell him to go outside?"

"Why didn't you?" Aiden suggested.

Justin looked over at the man standing with his back to the bar. "See what you mean. Don't think I'd argue with him."

"Thought you kept yourself fit, ready for anything."

"Not for that." Justin told Aiden. "Oh god, he's coming back."

The man was returning. There was an old fashioned tankard in one hand and two in another.

"One of cider, one of dark ale, is it not Sirs?"

He placed the two tankards down in front of them, the third he kept for himself. He dragged a chair up to the end of the table.

'Oh, god,' thought both Aiden and Justin, 'he's joining us.'

"Well now, me hearties, drink up those fancy glasses, then we can have a proper toast."

The man brought his tankard to his lips but his eyes were on the two of them.

"Come now," he said, "drink up. You can't expect me to drink alone now can you?"

Both of them gave him a weak smile, raised their glasses and downed the remains. Hopefully, they thought, once they had finished the drinks he'd bought them they could make an excuse and make their escape.

They each took a swig out of their tankards.

"Um, so," Aiden tried to make conversation, "what do you do?"

The man stared at him. "But I thought you'd guessed young Sir. Did you not call me 'mate'? I thought you had fathomed that I was a seaman."

"Ah, right, of course." Said Aiden, though not really sure what the man meant, but thought it would be best to simply agree to whatever he said; the less conversation they engaged in the sooner they'd be able to get away from him.

"Now," said the man, "a toast."

He raised his tankard. Without thinking Aiden and Justin did the same.

"To His Majesty the King and success against the Spanish."

And he took a deep draught from his tankard. But he still stared at the two of them over it.

They followed suit. Clearly the man was a bit deranged; he was living in another world, or another time. He didn't toast the Queen and what had the Spanish got to do with anything.

The man smiled at them and his gold tooth sparkled. "You have the better of me, young gentlemen. You know of my calling, but I do not know of yours."

Justin looked at Aiden. Aiden realised that he wanted him to speak.

"Justin is a businessman." He told the man. "Well, he is just starting up a business. I work for an investment firm. I'm advising him, helping him."

The man's eyes widened. "Young gentlemen of commercial enterprise is it? And a young man with investors as partners. I knew you were not men of a menial background as soon as I saw you. Mister Guy, I says to myself, these are young men of standing and education, just look at the way they are dressed, look at their soft hands, young men used to noble and respectable work, not one of hard graft. Not that hard graft ever hurt a man, and could not be just as noble. It is a pleasure to make myself acquainted with such venerable young men as the two of you. A toast!" he said. "A toast to my new found friends!"

Again he took a draught and again his piercing eyes looked at them over the rim of his tankard. So they drank. And their tankards were more than half empty.

The candle's flames quivered in a cold draught that flowed suddenly through the bar. Aiden and Justin looked to see if the door had opened and if more customers had come in. Mister Guy took no notice. The door had not opened, it had remained shut.

But to Aiden and Justin it looked as if the fog from outside had entered the pub, only faintly, but each could have sworn the floor had a film of mist over it. And the temperature had certainly dropped. Perhaps the central heating had gone off along with the electric.

"One last toast to my new young friends." said Mister Guy. "To you future success and happiness."

He raised his tankard and smiled at them.

'Good.' Thought both Aiden and Justin. 'A final drink and the strange man would leave them alone and be on his way.

They all drank back the remains of their tankards.

It was Aiden who first looked puzzled, and then Justin. Aiden tipped his now empty tankard up over the table. Something fell from it. Justin did the same, and another small object hit the table and rolled a little way before twirling to a stop.

From each tankard had fallen a coin.

They both picked up their coins and looked at them. They were small, looked old and shone in the light of the table's single candle.

"There now." Said Mister Guy. "A small recompense for your company and the time you have given me."

They both looked from the coins to Mister Guy. He was still smiling but no longer showing his teeth.

In the bar beyond Mister Guy's frame the mist was thickening, the detail of the bar becoming less distinct, only the yellow points of light showed where the candles burned. The world beyond Mister Guy was disappearing. Mister Guy was becoming the centre and only thing in their world and in their vision.

Aiden and Justin were both becoming sleepy; dizziness was enveloping them as the fog was enveloping the bar.

They both tried to stand, to get out of their chairs. They could not. They rose only a few inches and slumped back down again. Neither could find movement in their tongues, neither could form a word, and neither could speak to Mister Guy or to each other.

The fog closed around them. They slumped forward onto the table, asleep.

The pub's door opened. Four burly men entered. They headed straight for the table. Mister Guy stood and moved aside for them. Aiden and Justin. Were each taken by two men. They were lifted up and taken from the pub. Mister Guy followed.

They walked out into the street. It was foggy and dark. The pub did not look the same as it had done. The sign above it had changed. It was called 'The Admiral Benbow'. The streets were not lit by any electric lights, indeed they were not lit at all. The only light came from the windows of the buildings around; and they did not look as before either. The cobbles were the same but no cars rumbled across them, now it was carts and horses. And the quayside was no longer a home to boats that were restaurants and bars, now they were the berthing place of large sailing ships. The sounds, the smells, the sights, none of them were of the days belonging to Aiden or Justin. These were of days long past, as things were and used to be.

The party walked to a nearby ship and ascended the gangplank.

As soon as they were aboard it was taken away. The ship would be ready to sail in the morning.

-:-

It wasn't until the next afternoon that Aiden's manager at Woodes, Crispe and Colston became concerned that he had not turned up for work, neither was he answering his mobile. He found out from the security guard that Aiden was the last to leave the building the night before, signing out just before 7pm.

It was then that the receptionist received a call from a bed and breakfast establishment asking if Justin was at the office, having a meeting perhaps. When they had gone in to clean his room they realised had not used it the night before. There was a letter on his desk with their phone number on it, which is why they had called.

Aiden's manager decided to call the police.

Two days later there had still been no sign of them. The police had discovered that Justin had been to the gym and met Auden outside at 7pm; the gym had a security camera trained on the entrance. They had walked away together towards the area of bars and restaurants.

The police conducted enquiries throughout the area and found out that the two of them had been drinking in the Llandoger Trow. They had stayed there drinking for some time according to the barman, unfortunately because of a power cut; there were no security recordings of them leaving.

The police decided to use divers to search the waters around the nearby quayside. They were well aware of what might happen to young men who had been drinking too much. High spirits, in more way than one, could lead them to slipping and falling into the cold dark waters of the docks. And all too often they never came up again.

After a great deal of searching nothing was found.

One day perhaps, their bones may turn up, but it was doubtful. They were young men lost forever.

There were calls, as usual, for more money to be spent on safety measures, and more money would be spent, but more poor young souls would still be taken from us. No amount of money can keep everyone safe.

Planetarium

They had a minibus of children; thirteen year old school children. It was coming to the end of the school year and it was the time for annual trips; educational ones supposedly. The educationalists may think so, the teachers knew better. And the eighteen children knew better still; nine of them boys and nine girls, very non-discriminatory.

Christopher and Amanda - Mr Lewis and Miss Walker – shepherded the children of the coach. The driver had stopped to unload them on the main road as close as he could to their destination but would have to drive away and park elsewhere. He couldn't stop long where he was, it was designated as no parking, so he wanted them to hurry. The learners, as they were called these days, were gathered into as organised a group as possible and counted. Christopher, he preferred Chris, ticked and signed a pre-printed sheet on the clipboard he carried. Either he or Amanda would be counting, ticking and signing it regularly throughout the day. At no point must they miscount or lose a single individual. They would not move an inch away from any assembly point until the total was correct and every child was present in body in not wholly in   mind.

Along the side of the wide modern path were two large buildings each quite new. To the left of the children as they turned to look at them was an aquarium, a large building of red brick to one side and curved glass panels to the other with a curved and undulating glass roof. In front and to the right of the group was a large long glass fronted oblong of a building that housed a technology museum aimed at children. But neither of these were their destination. Theirs was on the other side of them in a large modern square once part of the old dockyards.

"Right! Quiet everyone! Quiet!" Chris shouted above the hubbub. "Remember what you've been told. Stick together at all times. No wandering off. Absolutely no wandering off for whatever reason. If it's the toilet you need you must ask myself or Miss Walker first."

Several hands were immediately raised. "Sir, Sir." "Miss, Miss." Was the chorus.

Chris sighed. "All right." He said. "After the journey the first stop is the toilets."

He looked at Amanda who was surveying the nearby signs.

"This way." She said. "They're on the way to the Planetarium anyway."

"Right everyone!" Chris called out. "Follow us, keep together, this way."

Chris led them and from amidst the chatter behind him he could hear the sighs. The children could not understand why he should treat them like children, they were thirteen now after all.

Chris and Amanda led them through a gap between the two large buildings. It opened out into a wider area with entrances to the aquarium and museum as well as a number of restaurants and cafes. They turned to their right which took them to the main square and, according to the signposts, the toilets. They were located underground along with a large car park.

Chris and Amanda led them down, waited outside both the gents and ladies for each of them to return, walked back up the steps to the main square, reorganised them, counted, ticked, and were happy that all were present and correct.

From the underground entrance they could look across the square. The square was wide and open. Modern water features had been implanted and some small children, their parents watching, played in a shallow pool that had behind it a wall of water cascading over burnished steel. Further ahead, close to the museum building, was the Planetarium.

It was a great mirrored ball. Panes of shaped mirrors adorned the entire structure like silver scales on a giant reptilian egg. Segments of the blue sky and patches of white clouds reflected from the upper sphere. On one side mirrored tesserae cast back the glass walls of the museum. The rest of the sphere took the scene of the square, its fountains and water, and the people within it, and cut it into fragments throwing them back at the originals.

The school group could see itself reflected. But the copy was cracked and splintered by the mirrors. In the eye of the sphere they were fragmented.

"That's it." announced Chris. "The Planetarium."

He heard several of them say 'cool'. One of the girls made an unnecessary and uncomplimentary remark about another's appearance, and they had all taken out their phones and were taking pictures of themselves taking pictures of themselves.

"We've got nearly half an hour before our booking." Said Amanda. "We may as well let them have their packed lunches before going in. There's plenty of room over there." She pointed to the stone surrounds of poorly planted flower beds that looked fine to use as seating. "We'll be close enough to the Planetarium entrance when our booking's due."

Chris agreed, organised the children and they traipsed over to the improvised seating.

Chris wasn't really hungry so strolled over to the Planetarium entrance. Metal steps led up to a door. It was a solid steel door buffed to shiny surface like the mirrored walls. He ascended the steps and tried the door. It was firmly shut. He went back down. As he did so a man approached.

"You must be the school party." He said.

"Uh, yes that's us." Chris nodded over to the children eating their sandwiches.

The man smiled. A gold tooth sparkled in the light reflected by the sphere.

"I'll be ready for you when you're ready." He said.

"Oh, right, well, as soon as they've finished their lunch I'll bring them over."

"Perfect." said the man flashing another smile.

Within twenty minutes everyone had finished their lunch. In fact, they had finished lunch, got bored, messed about, chattered, giggled, and even let of a loud scream.

Chris shouted and demanded order and told them to put all their rubbish into the nearby bins or into their backpacks and return it home. Eventually a relative quite descended on them. Amanda and Chris counted, ticked and signed the sheet on the clipboard. It was time for the Planetarium.

They walked across their end of the square to it. As they neared the man appeared from behind it and waited by the steps.

"Good morning." He said looking at his watch. Two minutes to twelve. It was till morning. "Welcome to the Planetarium."

The murmuring form the children died away as the man's gaze fell upon them. He smiled again and his tooth sparkled. To the children, and to Amanda, he was handsome for someone of his age, although it was difficult to tell what that was. His skin was smooth and glowed in the reflected light of the sphere. His hair was black but had streaks of grey on the sides which might have been premature. There was one thing, as far as the children were concerned, his presence was far more commanding than Mr Lewis.

Chris rummaged in a shoulder bag for the paperwork.

"Please." said the man holding out his hand towards Chris. "That won't be necessary. I know who you are. You are not likely to be another such group at exactly the same time are you?" He paused and smiled again.

Chris smiled in return and withdrew his hand.

"Eighteen children and two adults isn't it? Half male, half female." "Um, yes, twenty altogether, that's right." Agreed Chris, though thinking it odd that he called them male and female.

"Well then," said the man opening the door, "everyone, please enter for your Planetarium experience."

Amanda and Chris went first and the children filed passed the smiling man.

It was as large inside as they had imagined from the outside. Tiers of seats were arranged in a semi circle. There was easily room for more than twice their number. The chairs were like those in cinemas but could lean further back and there was more leg room between them. The audience could lie back and see the story of the stars, galaxies and universe unfold across the ceiling as if it were the night sky.

They were all in and the children competed for seats. Why it should be a competition when there were more than enough seats for twice their number was for the children to know and not for the adults to understand.

The man closed the door firmly behind him.

The lighting was dim as it was in a cinema before the start of a film.

"Please." Said the man his voice rising above those of the children and immediately demanding their attention. "Make yourselves comfortable. The exposition is in 3D, you will find glasses under each seat for you to wear. The story of this planet and star and that of the galaxy and the wonders of the universe will unfold before your eyes with such realism you might swear that you yourselves were actually on such a journey through space and time."

Quietness and expectation fell upon them as the man retreated through an internal door to a control room to begin the show.

The dim lights faded and the darkness of night entered the auditorium.

The show began.

The sky at night. The stars as they would have been seen at this very location on a cloudless night if not one beam of artificial light had invaded and rubbed the things that might have been seen. It was the night sky as it truly was, and truly should be.

The soundtrack told them of our own sun and the planets orbiting around it. It took them on a journey as if on a space craft from one planet to the next, from Mercury to Pluto, exploring each of them in 3D and in the detail of the very latest data available. It did so transcending time, at a speed faster than light would have travelled from Sol to the outer fringes of its empire. The three dimensions of the solar system surpassed by the fourth.

The children were transfixed as were Amanda and Chris.

Then the soundtrack told them they would go beyond the solar system. They would travel to stars near and far and they would stop at planets, extra-terrestrial worlds. New worlds were being discovered every day by astronomers, it seemed that almost any star might have planets around it. But they would not all be suitable for human life. The search was on, however, and one day, maybe soon, earth-like planets would be found.

Let us imagine their discovery.

The journey was through a light swarm of stars. In the centre of their vision was a single spot of light. The stars around it moved to the left and right, upward and downward. The star in the centre grew in brilliance. The other stars around it dimmed in its light. Now the night sky was of the central star itself with just a speckling of pinpricks filling the remaining space.

Suddenly into view grew a large planet, a gas giant. They skimmed passed it almost touching the yellow and green clouds that whirled over it.

They raced towards the star. Another planet loomed, bare of clouds, no sign of blue water, a brown-grey rock of a world.

And then in the distance a third planet appeared.

They slowed as they came towards it.

The sun in the distance was much like the star they had seen in the solar system, much like Sol. And the world they now saw was much like earth. Clouds swirled in patterns over half of it, though of a pink hue rather than the pure white clouds of Earth. And the oceans were also like those of Earth but less blue, they were made of waters tinged with purple.

They slowed to an orbit and watched the clouds, land and seas pass below them.

'Let us descend to this newly discovered world.' Said the commentary in much the same voice as that of the man in the control room.

Slowly they descended.

The planet was no longer an orb, its horizon was now a circle spreading out around them.

'Let us look at this alien landscape.' There is water, there is air, air that is breathable. Exotic plants cover much of the landmass, Small animals inhabit the ground.'

The view took then over an ocean towards land just north of the planet's equator. They came to a landmass. Coming over it they slowed and descended further. The land below was covered in strange looking trees, or what passed for trees here on this world. They were more like giant varieties of rhubarb, all different colours and shades although predominately of reds and light pinks.

The land rose as they moved away from the coast and the rhubarb tress became smaller and less numerous. Areas of open space appeared between them covered in mound of moss-like vegetation, again in the same shades of red and pink but with splashed of deep blue amongst them. The land flattened and became a plain. Small beasts ran fast over it, blue haired and with six legs. Other sphere shaped creatures seemed to roll across the plain like balls of fluff, animals with no apparent legs.

Small clumps of the trees appeared on the plain and between them rivers flowed and lakes sat lazily in depressions.

Through it all the children and the teachers were equally awestruck.

Their view slowed, almost hovering above the ground, above a clearing the clumps of trees close to a languid river.

'Let us take a close look at our surroundings.' Said the commentary.

Slowly the view descended until they looked at the scene as if standing on the ground.

There was a deep low thud. The viewers could feel it through the comfort of their chairs.

'We are here.' Said the voice. 'Let us experience this alien world.'

There was a hissing sound and a clunk.

The lights brightened to the low level they had been at the start.

Many of the children groaned. They had thought and hoped that the experience would continue, that the session would not be over. They wanted to see more. What they had seen had whetted their appetite. They yearned to know more.

After the sound of the hiss and clunk a crack appeared around d the door letting in bright sunlight. Slowly the door swung open.

Despite their enthusiasm for the show the children, as children do, had as much enthusiasm for something new. Once something was over it was over. Now was the time to move on.

Without instruction the children leapt from their seats, grabbed their bags, took the 3D glasses as a souvenir and headed for the door, all before the teachers could say anything.

"Slow down!" Chris called out o them.

"And wait for us outside, at the foot of the steps!" Amanda added.

Chris and Amanda rose from their seats and went to the control room door to thanks the man for giving them such a great experience. Chris knocked on it and said, "Excuse me."

He waited and knocked again. "Excuse me can we have a quick word?" he asked.

All the children had now left.

A single head peered back through the door. It was one of the boys.

"Sir! Sir!" Miss! You've got to see this! It's unbelievable! Quickly!"

And his head disappeared outside again.

The control room door didn't open.

Chris sighed. "We'd better see what mischief they've got up to." He told Amanda, and they left the control room door and went to the exit.

They looked out through the door.

They stared. They looked around at the outside of the Planetarium.

Before them was the scene they had stared at inside minutes before. It was not the square the Planetarium had stood in.

"Jesus Christ!" exclaimed Chris.

"This isn't possible." Said Amanda surprisingly quietly.

Chris turned and ran back to the control room door. Amanda hesitated. She called out to the children.

"Back! All of you! Now! Get back inside here, now!"

She turned and ran over the Chris who was banging on the control room door again and shouting for the man to come out.

There was a hissing sound.

Amanda turned to the exit door.

It was swinging shut.

"No!" She screamed, and ran towards it.

The door swung and before she could reach it she heard the clunk of it fully closing. There was another hiss like that of a seal being made. She screamed and banged on the door. Chris was still shouting and banging on the control room door.

The lights began to dim.

Chris and Amanda both fell silent and automatically turned to face the view of the alien world. On it they could see children running about. They could hear the sound of their laughing and calling out to each other, investigating the wonders of their new world.

When the lights had dimmed there was only the view of the alien world.

There was a slight thud which vibrated through the floor.

The teachers stared at the scene. They were unable to speak. The view was beginning to recede, they were leaving it, moving away, returning the way they had come.

Chris and Amanda ran to the control room door. They shouted, screamed and banged, and behind them the journey they had taken was being shown in reverse. They had left the alien world and its sun. They fell back through the field of stars. They skimmed passed the outer planets of Sol. They returned.

-:-

The police were trying to control some frightened parents. A few had rushed to the scene when told that their dear children were, for the time being, reported as missing.

The parents were demanding to know how it had happened, where had the teachers been, what had they been doing, where were they now?

They were in police custody. They were sat, handcuffed, in a police car.

The DI scratched his head and his Sergeant stared at the Planetarium.

"Children don't just disappear into thin air Sir." The Sergeant told his boss.

"Of course not." Sniffed the DI. "And there are only two people who can tell us what happened, and they seem to be struck dumb."

"Have you tracked down the manager he must have something to do with this?" The DI added looking up at the Planetarium.

"No Sir, he seems to have vanished as well."

"What was his name? "Guy, Sir, Mr Guy."

"Get an APW issued. I want him found. And I don't want him skipping the country."

Pier Island

The new apartments had been built on a small island together with a couple of cafes and a restaurant. It was connected to the shore by a causeway, not long but enough to separate it from the day to day activities of the mainland, separate but not isolated. The causeway was the width of a path and a two lane road that led to the development. The planners had not accounted for the amount of parking that residents would need which resulted in residents parking cars along one lane of the road making it basically single track.

The buildings rose from the rocky outcrop like some sort of ancient castle. Its walls were made of grey stone which so often reflected the colour of the sky and the water. The estuary in which it stood was tidal and had the greatest rise and fall of any, When the tide was out the island was like a beached whale upon a wide expanse of sand and mud, when it was in, but for the causeway, it would have been completely cut off.

It was a popular spot in the summer and residents shared their island village with holiday makers to the main resort that spread along an almost straight arc of beach interrupted by a large pier, a man-made reflection of the island, and other amusements. It was the price one paid for living there and if anyone felt they should complain they would be reminded that they should not have bought a home there in the first place.

It was a place to share with others; at least in the summer, but not so much in the winter. That was when the skies darkened and drew closer to the sea, and when the colour of both was almost indistinguishable. Winds would bring clouds, showers and days of rain which could be tracked in their march up the estuary and watched as the black veils of rain joined the clouds with the sea and either passed harmlessly by or enveloped the island and resort in the shroud.

And when, in the autumn, the air was still and cold, mist and fog would roll in form the open sea and blanket the buildings and their inhabitants.

Sarah and Joshua (Josh or JJ to his friends) had bought their first flat here on a whim. They had been living together in a rented flat for four years and, upon her grandfather's death, Sarah inherited enough money for a deposit on a home of their own. With both of their incomes they would be paying no more in a monthly mortgage than they were paying in rent to a landlord.

Sarah, particularly, thought it was an exciting and dramatic place to live and their friends would be envious. Josh wasn't so sure, he would have preferred the normality of a house, a garage and a garden in a road a few doors away from a local pub. But it was Sarah's money that paid the deposit and Sarah's choice that prevailed.

They moved in to their new home in late September, The summer weather had been rather wet and cool but there was a sudden change as they moved in and the resort was bathed in the warm light of an Indian Summer. It lasted more than two weeks. It made their new home on the island seem like the perfect place to live, the ideal choice. Sarah knew she had been right.

After the two weeks of idyllic weather it changed and in October a deep high pressure brought in cold air and with it frost and fog. But the days were still bright and cloudless and sat before a roaring fire at night – Sarah had insisted on a log burner which presented some logistical problems in procurement and delivery – the idyll continued.

The Thursday came when it was Josh's birthday but because they both had an early start in the morning and Sarah had a meeting in Bristol and would not be back until late, Sarah decided they must celebrate it on the Friday night. Josh wasn't so keen, he would sooner have met up with his mates from the local rugby club as usual but, as he knew, his life would not be worth living for a week or so if he declined the idea.

Sarah booked an Italian restaurant. There wasn't much of a variety of good restaurants in the resort. Its offerings were almost entirely aimed at day trippers and long-standing visits by families from the Midlands and South Wales, and then only in the summer. Much of the resort shut down after the season ended; the owners of hotels, B&B's and the like flying off for their own sun-kissed holidays abroad. Burgers and fish and chips with a sprinkling of old fashioned 'English' cafes, mostly run by second generation Italians and Greeks, filled the needs and stomachs of the visitors if not the residents.

They had a reasonable meal, a drink to start, a bottle of wine, and a couple of drinks afterwards. Josh still felt reasonably sober but it was more than enough for Sarah. And he had to hold on to a giggling companion all the way back to the causeway.

When they had arrived at the restaurant it had been misty, by the time they left a fog had rolled in from the sea. The yellow of the street lights bathed the fog and the streets in their glow, and with the lights from the shop windows the fog did not seem as dense as it would have done without them.

They left the town's streets and reached the esplanade. The only lights here were those of the main road, whiter and more widely spaced. And there was no protection for the full effect of the icy fog drifting in form the estuary. There was no wind and tide was in so the waves lapped only languidly against the shoreline. Josh raised his collar against the cold and did the same for Sarah although she seemed unaware of it. They were not too far from the causeway but Sarah made their progress slow and Josh wanted to get back into the warm so egged her on.

They came to the turning off the main road that was the causeway.

The fog had thickened as they approached their turning. Josh could see tarmac and the white dashes of the central line nut not much else either side. As far as looking ahead was concerned it was a blank wall of white. It should be very dark but the white of the fog glowed with both the moonlight and the few lights that ran along the road. He and Sarah would have to follow the centre of the road. It would be safe enough; he could not imagine any cars venturing out into such a pea-souper.

Step by step they walked forward. Sarah was now more aware than when they had left the restaurant, the cold air must have cleared her head.

Josh lost track of the white dashes. Perhaps they did not run all the way along the road to the island, he had never taken any notice of them before. They had not bumped into any of the parked cars on the left side and had not come against the kerb on the right so they were on track and would soon be on the island and home.

The tarmac became very gritty. The council must have put salt and grit on it expecting ice by morning.

At last the road was a cobbled surface. They had reached the open courtyard in front of the apartments, buildings and cafes. It was difficult to judge the direction but Josh was sure the door to their apartment was just to the right. They turned that way.

A soft breeze blew from the sea and the fog began to thin. Both of them were relieved, at last they would be able to see exactly where they were.

The fog was quickly clearing. They had taken the correct direction. A building loomed before them. They looked for the door. Both Josh and Sarah frowned. They looked at the wall in front of them. They looked up at it and to the left then to the right. It was not the apartment block.

In fact it was no building they had seen before. It was not one of the island buildings they knew so well.

It was grey stone, granite, but it was old, rough, weathered and stained. There was no door in front of them and it had only small windows high above the ground. It looked like an old warehouse.

"Where the hell is this? You must have taken a wrong turning." scolded Sarah.

"I could have sworn I didn't." replied Josh, frowning and still looking at the building.

The fog was clearing even more. They could see this building and more. Beyond them was greyness. All of the buildings were old and dilapidated.

"Let's go back." Sarah said with a shiver. "I don't like this."

"Right, yeah, we'll go back." Agreed Josh in a quiet and guarded voice. "Let me just take a look over there first." He added, pointing out at the greyness.

"Oh, Josh, can't we just go."

"It won't take a moment, and then we'll go back. The fog's going now anyway."

Sarah sighed and pulled her coat more closely to her. It seemed colder now than when they'd been in the fog.

She followed Josh as he went off towards the grey.

They came to a low stone way. Josh stopped and looked beyond it. It was grey, but two shades of grey. It was a grey he had seen enough times before, half was that of the sky and half of the water. And the sound that reached his ears was that of the lapping waves.

He looked back at the old buildings they'd just discovered.

"There's something wrong here." He said.

"I don't like it here," said Sarah, "come on let's go, let's go back."

Josh's mouth had gone dry and he felt perspiration on his brow despite the cold.

"It's the island." He said.

"Yes, let's get back there. Let's go Josh; now."

"No." said Josh firmly. "This is the island."

"Don't be stupid Josh, this isn't it. It doesn't look anything like this. Stop messing about. I'm cold and I've had enough. I'm going."

Sarah pulled the coat even tighter and stomped off, as best her shoes would allow on the cobbles, to the road.

Josh stared at the buildings a moment longer then quickly followed her.

He caught up with her and took hold of her arm to slow her down.

"Please Josh, let's just get back."

"Sorry Sarah. It's just ... well, it's just like this is the island. But what it was like before the apartments were built."

"Josh!" Sarah said sternly in the school-teacherly way she had a habit of using if she thought he was wrong or if his decisions did not fit with hers. "These are not our apartments. This is not the island. You just have to look at it to see that. Now, come on, let's find that road and get back."

She turned and headed to the road. Josh said nothing and followed.

Josh noticed that here the road was cobbled in the way the courtyard was. A heavy mist still clung to it and Sarah strode off along it and into the mist. Josh was just behind her.

Within a few meters the mist was thickening again into a fog. Sarah stumbled on the cobbles and Josh took her arm. This was not the road as Josh remembered it; cobbles not tarmac.

The fog embraced them. Only the light of a full moon brightened the gloom and gave the fog a sheen.

"I don't believe it. It's as thick here as it was before." said Josh.

"Just keep going," Demanded Sarah, "A few more meters and we'll be at the main road."

As quickly as the fog had thickened it now dispersed. It faded into a mist. They stopped. They looked. Before them was not the main road but buildings, somehow different to the ones before but very similar; and old. It was as if they had come around in a circle and ended up where they had started.

"We're back there." whispered Josh.

"Back where?" asked Sarah in a more uncertain tome than before. "It's not the same place. Those buildings are different."

"But it's not the main road or the town is it? If it's not, then where is it? Where else can it be? We didn't walk far down that road."

"But that's simply not possible. And it doesn't look the same."

Josh began to walk slowly towards the buildings, and then he stopped. There were lights in some windows. He heard people's voices and music, what sounded like an accordion.

"Let's ask someone where we are, ask them for directions." suggested Sarah.

"No." Josh said firmly. "I don't think we should do that."

"Why ever not? We just need someone to show us the way home."

Josh started to walk to the greyness to the left of the buildings.

Sarah let out a deep breath. "Josh," she shouted at him, "I was talking to you!"

He stopped at the stone wall. Beyond were the greys of the sea and the sky and above the sounds from the buildings was that of the lapping waves.

Josh stared down at the water. "It's the island." He said.

"Josh." Sarah said coming beside him and taking an arm. "What is it? What is going on? I don't like it. You're not just playing some stupid game are you? Trying to scare me or something. Please Josh let's just stop this and go back home."

He stared into her eyes. She could see that it was not only her who was worried and a little scared.

"I'm not playing any games Sarah. This is nothing to do with me. Something's going on. I don't know what it is and I don't like it either. And, at the moment, I don't know what to do about it."

"Please Josh, let's go back down the road and get back home."

He took both of her arms. "I'm worried," he said, "that if we try again we still won't get back home. We might be even further away."

Sarah shook her head. "Josh, you're just talking nonsense. We've got to try and get through that fog again. Just one more time. We've got to try. Just for me. Please."

Josh took a deep breath. "OK." He agreed. "Once more"

He had agreed because she was pleading with him, but also because of another feeling, a feeling of curiosity, of wanting to find out what would happen, where they would be if they tried just one more time.

They set off. Again as they walked along the road the light mist turned to dense fog. Again they did not emerge onto the main road nor see the lights of the town ahead of them. Instead they emerged as they had done before, on the island.

But again the buildings were different. Stone had been replaced by wood. Large wooden houses stood around an open central area. The cobbles underfoot were now rough pebbles, sand and mud. Smoke drifted from the centre of the roofs and was captured in a layer by the mist. Dull yellow light pierced through the gaps in the windows and the edges of the doors. The ground of the central area was wet and muddy. Some chickens wandered between the buildings and the smell of the estuary was covered by the smells of the farmyard.

Josh turned away from the settlement and walked to the waterside. No longer was it bounded by stone blacks. Now there was just the natural rock of the island.

"We've gone back in time." said Josh.

Sarah stared at him, bemused.

He continued. "Each time we try to get through the fog we go back in time."

Sarah shook her head. "That's not possible. It's impossible."

"Then you explain it!" Josh almost shouted.

"There's no need to be like."

Josh sighed. "All I'm asking it that you come up with some other explanation. I can't."

He turned and looked back towards the houses

"But how do we get back?" Sarah asked wearily as if accepting what he said or being too tired or upset to think of anything else.

Josh took his turn to shake his head. "I don't know."

"Do we just wait until morning?" Sarah asked. "What if the fog disappears, what them? Don't say we'll be stuck here. Don't say we can't get back! We have to get back!"

Tears were welling up in her eyes.

Josh grabbed her and hugged her tightly. "It's OK, it's OK. We won't get stuck here, we'll get back. I promise you."

He pulled back and kissed her forehead.

"But how?" she asked. "How can you promise?"

"I need to think. Let me think about it. I'll come up with a plan. It'll be all right, you'll see."

Staring out at the grey sea and sky Josh tried to think. He tried but his mind was blank. It was not as if he had any spark of an idea. In fact he did not think about what to do about what had happened only the fact that it had happened. His mind was not giving away any answers. It was as if he had a simple fatalistic acceptance of their position; what will be will be. Whatever they did, whatever plan they might have had, it would make no difference. His brain was in limbo, much as they were.

"One more time" Sarah broke into his reverie. "Just one more time. We have to try. Maybe the fog will lift." She looked up at him with pleading eyes.

'Maybe the fog will lift.' Thought Josh. 'Maybe then I can think of something.'

He shrugged. What was there to lose; nothing. In which case there may be a gain. "OK, just one more time." He agreed.

Once more onto the road, which was now just a track. Once more into the mist and then the fog. Once more the fog cleared, and once more they were on the island.

The buildings were gone. At least they could see no buildings within the mist. The track, once a road, was now not more than a path, a well trodden line across the sparsely covered ground. To begin with the island looked empty. But, through the mist there was a yellow glow, a single light, perhaps a fire. It must be a fire for Josh and Sarah could both smell the smoke that had risen from it and then descended to the ground.

They both shivered.

"We've gone too far." Said Josh. "We shouldn't have done it, shouldn't have tried again."

"This just cannot be happening!" said Sarah with a sob.

"But it is."

"What the hell are we going to do?" Sarah demanded.

Josh looked back along the path. The wall of mist and then fog started a little way along it.

"We can't keep going back." He said.

He looked towards the light of the fire in the mist.

"There's nothing for it." He said. "We'll have to see who's there."

"Are you sure? I'm not sure we should."

"Nothing else for it. What else can we do?"

Sarah took his arm with both of hers and held him tightly. She took a deep breath. "Ok." She said quietly.

They began walking towards the light. As they did so the mist cleared. The light was indeed a fire. Flames licked upward from a pile of burning logs. Nearby was a tent of some description. Hanging over the fire on metal legs was a cooking pot. A man sat on the other side of the fire. His face burned with the firelight. He was clean shaven and his blue-black eyes reflected the dancing flames. They could see he had black wavy hair. He was watching them. As they came closer he stood.

As soon as Josh and Sarah saw what he wore they recognised what he was. He was a Roman soldier, a Centurion.

He smiled and walked around the fire towards them. As he came in front of the fire and was outlined by it as a dark shape his hand went to his side. The moonlight was strong and they could now see his face in ghostly white. He smiled. A single gold tooth sparkled in the moonlight. His hand moved from his side and as it did so there was the slicing sound of metal. As his arm rose they could see that he held a sword. Josh and Sarah heard what sounded like a laugh. The man moved forward, coming at them.

Josh and Sarah moved at the same time. Josh shouted 'run' and they both did, towards the path and the mist and fog. They no longer clung to each other.

Josh entered the fog. He had heard Sarah running, she was close behind him. The fog deadened the sounds. Josh slowed breathing heavily. He turned. Sarah should be close behind him. But she wasn't. She didn't appear through the fog. He had heard her running, her footsteps. He called out, shouted out her name. She must have fallen.

Fear and cold flooded through him. He shouted again, screamed, and then started running back the way he had come. She must be on the path, she had to be, she had only been a few meters behind him.

The fog cleared. Light mist replaced it.

In front of him was the main road.

In front of him the lights and the buildings of the town. The town as it should have been, as it was.

He turned back. He must go back, through the mist and fog. He could not stay here. He had to find Sarah. He had to rescue her.

But the fog was lifting, clearing; a breeze was blowing in from the sea. The road and the causeway were now visible as were the island and lights of the apartment buildings.

He had lost her.

-:-

The Corners Court gave an open verdict. They had no evidence as to how Sarah Thomas had disappeared or what had become of her. No body was ever discovered. At first Josh was the main suspect but no evidence was found either on him or in their apartment to suggest any foul play. The only thing the Police had uncovered was that they had been drinking quite heavily at a nearby restaurant, confirmed by the management. The final assumption was that she had fallen into the water whilst drunk, which was when Joshua had raised the alarm. Joshua was affected so tragically by what happened he was admitted to a mental hospital. It was odd that her body was never recovered; it could surely not have gone far.

Class Reunion

It was 2006. William had started his new job the year before. He worked for a regeneration scheme in an inner city area. Their main office was housed in an old Victorian junior school; a new one had been built nearby with regeneration funding. A local office providing support for the residents of the area was based in one of the 1960's row of shops that the council had built when they had previously tried to renew the area by demolishing the old back-to-back Victorian housing, which they considered to bordering on slums, for modern, concrete, up to date tower blocks of flats.

Having set up another regeneration scheme some forty years afterward was, to many, obviously an admission of failure. Not that it was one the council would have admitted to. They would not be demolishing these flats, they would be refurbishing them; and building less tall blocks filling in the spaces which until now were grassed areas. The area would be more people friendly and safer with the introduction of a large number of security cameras covering every corner of the estate with a central control room whose screens would be monitored by eagle-eyed security guards twenty four hours a day seven days a week. Mr George Orwell would have been impressed.

But William would have to admit that the politics of the projects which had at first interested him no longer did.

He would go over to the local office quite regularly for one reason or another; perhaps to attend a meeting, to deliver documents or to pick some up. A new young woman, Jenifer, had recently joined the staff and they had given her a desk in the office. She was there primarily to give IT support to both that office and the main one but also to help local residents wanting to use two public computers with internet connection that were place in the entrance of the office; a useful and necessary toll these days when completing many of the Council's online forms and applications for housing and other benefits.

William had always been involved in IT both for work and as a hobby and was considered a bit of a whiz with some of the more intricate software packages himself. It was natural that he should get into a conversation with her.

It wasn't long before he found out that she was the daughter of one of his old school friends whom he'd lost contact with over the years. In fact he'd lost contact with all but one of them, John, and even he was no longer what one would call a close friend. William passed on his name and details for Jenifer to give to her father, Robert, thinking it may be a good idea if they met up sometime.

During the next couple of days he began wondering what had happened to the other class-mates and couldn't resist trying to find out. It was becoming much easier with the trails people left on social media and other sites. In a short time he had located another one, Patricia. She had married before the friends had all taken different paths, and in fact they had all attended her wedding to Steven, she was the first of them to be married. Since then William discovered that she had become a Methodist Minister and lived in a village to the south of Birmingham. He was able to use the church web site to contact her.

She soon replied and thought that it would be a great idea if all the old friends could be found and then they could get together and have a reunion. By then Jenifer's father Robert had also got back to him with the same idea. He had heard that another of the gang, Richard, had moved to Gloucester and had married another of the group, Susan.

William searched online and up popped Richard's name and his business. He was a dealer in antique books. A far cry from anything William could remember about him. But, using the email address he contacted him and, within a day, another gang member was all up for a reunion.

One more friend remained and it only by chance that William found him. It was not the internet that provided the answer this time but the local newspaper. He happened to glance at an article to do with a nearby railway seaside station and noticed the Station Manager's name. It was their old comrade.

It had only taken a couple of weeks and the group of friends were back in contact with each other.

William, having instigated the whole affair, was the one who had to arrange a date, time and place for a reunion acceptable to everyone. Some of the old friends would be staying overnight, some coming by train – the Station Master having concessionary tickets - and he and John living on the outskirts of the city could meet up almost anywhere.

They would want somewhere where they could easily talk, somewhere to sit and eat and, most importantly, drink. A private function room would be the answer. William mulled it over. He wanted somewhere different, not just the usual pub or restaurant. The answer came to him.

In the old city docks was berthed a famous old steam ship. It was the original iron steamship to cross the Atlantic from England to Americas in a style that had previously been unheard of, and with engines that made the crossing faster than any before. Now, after a long period of restoration, it was in dry dock. The renovations were ongoing but complete enough to make it a new tourist attraction.

The Ships owners now hired out the old first class dining room for parties and corporate functions. It would be ideal, but maybe a bit pricey. Luckily for William his boss, the Director of the Charity, had a contact, one of the Directors of the Trust that managed the steamship. And he in his turn could talk to the General Manager and see if a deal could be done. It also helped that on hearing who the group was the Director of the Trust admitted to being an old boy of their Grammar School himself, although not a contemporary; he would put some extra pressure on the General Manager on their behalf.

In the end the price was no more than they would have paid for a room in a pub or restaurant and they would be getting first class service and food.

The date was set. The reunion would be on the second Saturday in November.

Being a Friday evening and most of them travelling after work there wasn't time for all of them to meet up beforehand. The first time that they would meet after all the years since their school days would be when they arrived at the ship; except, that is, for William and John. Still being locals they had time to have a drink at a nearby local pub before everyone else arrived.

Clouds were coming in on a strengthening wind off the Severn estuary. The sun set at its preordained time but darkness seemed to descend before the time appointed. There was a spit or two of rain in the air.

William and John drank a pint at the Crown and Sceptre until it was time to go the short distance to the dry dock and the entrance to the ship. There would be about half an hour before any of the others were due to arrive but it wouldn't have surprised them if someone turned up early.

The general manager was waiting for them and escorted them through the ticket office to the ship's gangplank and then on board. He was an elegant man with dark wavy hair, bright eyes and a ready smile. He handed them over to the events manager who took them down to the dining room and proudly showed them the table and settings. Both were duly impressed, the staff had gone to a great deal of trouble and everything looked magnificent; as it would have done at the height of first class Atlantic travel.

A call came from the deck. The first of the guests were arriving. William went back on deck to meet the, John staying in the dining room ready to greet and offer drinks.

First to arrive were Robert and Mary, Jenifer's parents. The rest of them followed quickly; Patricia, the minister, and her husband Steven, Susan and Richards, the married classmates, and finally David and his Wife Barbara. David was the final member that William had managed to contact. When he had left school he had gone to theatre school, not to become an actor but to study stage design and was now working in a provincial theatre in the north of England.

William had taken each arrival down to the dining room and out of the worsening weather where John could ply them with aperitifs.

The inital drink became more than one; there was much to talk about after all the years apart. But the timetable for the meal must be kept, the chef had it all planned and timed and did not like any deviation from it. The events manager, acting as the maitre d', was politely insistent enough to get them to their seats as the first course was arriving.

Bottles of wine also arrived, opened and poured. The party was already getting merry. The guests were in good spirits in more way than one and the starter had been excellent, everyone passing on their compliments to the chef.

The main course arrived and was especially impressive, and it came with yet more bottles of wine.

Each of the group was the telling the others of their lives since leaving school. What was intriguing was that, despite all leaving the same school at the same time with much the same qualifications, how their lives ah diverged. There could hardly be a greater variation in careers, in successes and setbacks, and in the perceptions of each other and where their lives would have taken them when they were just eighteen years old. Not one of them would have guessed what the other had done or had become except perhaps for David who had always had a desire to work in art and the theatre, had done so, and remained so.

By the time the dessert arrived the atmosphere might have been what is was when they were eighteen, gathered together in the first local pub that would believe, or care, that they were old enough to drink, although it would have taken far less that tonight's tally of drinks to have affected them to the same degree. But despite the ability of their age to consume greater amounts of alcohol they were now getting somewhat drunk.

The dessert plates were cleared away. The kitchen could close down and the events manager could, after providing some more bottles of wine, retire to his office on the dockside. He could return at 2am to ensure they left or had left and lock up.

A large and of-the-period clock was hung at the opposite end of the dining room to the stairs up to the deck. The second hand was sweeping towards midnight. There was loud laughter from the gathered classmates as they recalled the mischief and scrapes that they had got into and the many shenanigans that had got up to which they believed had never been noticed.

The teachers noticed of course, but it was at that time when the new cohorts of them were a post war generation and although they had signed up to teach at a grammar school they had been imbued from their training that a more egalitarian and comprehensive system of education was inevitable. They lacked the simple discipline of the old guard, the teachers that still reigned supreme in the staff room. Consequently they turned a blind eye to much of the misbehaviour.

The second hand reached the pinnacle of its circular route. It was midnight.

David had not joined in quite as enthusiastically as the others in either laughter or alcohol. It was he who first felt the vibration. He could have sworn that there was a throbbing coming from beneath the floor. He felt his chair and the table. Hi listened closely trying to cut out the noise of the others. It was in his feet that he felt the rhythmic throb most clearly. It definitely came from below.

In a lull between the talk and laughter he pointed it out to the others.

"It must be the coolers in a cellar for the bar. They can make quite a bit of noise sometimes." said John knowingly. He considered himself something of an expert on licensed premises, and with good reason.

The others listened. They too could hear it and feel in beneath their feet.

"Air conditioning." said Robert decisively. "It'd be pretty stuffy in here without it."

The matter concluded to their satisfaction more drinks were poured.

David still thought it odd but tried to cast it from his mind and accepted a top-up.

The talking continued.

There was a louder thud.

David noticed it. The others seemed not to.

He felt a stronger throbbing coming from the floor. He was sure it could not be coolers or air conditioning. This vibration was much stronger.

David raised his voice. "It's not air conditioning. You can really feel it now. It's getting louder."

It was true, it was now quite loud and the vibrations thudded through the floor into their feet and up their legs. They could feel it through their chairs.

William frowned. "It's like a ship's engines."

"No engine on this ship. Not now at any rate." said Richard.

"An effect." Robert suggested. "Makes it feel like the real thing, like you're really on board a ship. Pretty effective I'd say. A damn good effect."

"Why would they put it on now?" asked Susan.

Robert shrugged. "To make us feel like it's the real thing, like we're on the real ship."

"What, after midnight?" she asked.

"Ah the witching hour!" exclaimed Robert. "Trying to get us scared!"

"Pretty silly if you ask me." Sniffed Barbara dismissively.

There was another thud and a jolt.

The glasses on the table wobbled some of them spilling wine.

"What the hell!" said William.

"Don't like the sound of that." added John.

"That's no air conditioner." Robert deduced.

"Whatever it is, it sounds dangerous!" Barbara exclaimed.

"Perhaps we'd better leave." David suggested.

"Sounds a good idea to me. Let's go." Agreed William.

They were about to stand but had not left their seats. They felt the room sway to the left and slowly to the right,.

They stared at each other, each sobering up.

"What the hell ...." Robert began.

From the right hand side the room swayed again. It tipped forward then, slowly, eased back, and then back further.

"My god, Steven, what's going on!" demanded Patricia.

"This can't be happening." William said holding on to the side of the table. "We're fixed to a dry dock. We can't be moving."

The others just stared at each other clinging on to either the table or the arms of the chairs.

"Well, it is happening." David told them. "And it's no effect. It can't be an effect. And I know about effects in the theatre."

"If it's not an effect." Asked Robert, "what is it.?"

"If it's not an effect," David told him, and the others, "it can only be real."

The room suddenly pitched forward again.

Both Patricia and Barbra let out screams. Susan grabbed hold of Richard and Mary, Robert's wife, clung terrified to the chair with a look of frozen panic.

The room moved. There was no doubt now in some minds what the movements were. They were the movements of a ship at sea.

"I'm going on deck." Said William making a decision.

"I'll go with you." David told him.

"OK," William agreed. "The rest of you stay here. We'll see what all this is about."

"Are you sure?" Barbara asked.

"Someone has to do something." David told her. "We can't just sit here."

"Be careful." Barbara added, fear in her eyes.

William and David left their chairs and walked unsteadily to the stairs, the floor beneath them moving one way then the other.

William took the lead and ascended the stairs keeping a firm grip on the handrails. He opened the door to the deck.

The night was dark. He felt the sting and cold of rain on his cheeks. The wind blew much harder than before, it felt like a gale. The rain now fell in sheets. Above him were not the empty masts of the ship in dock bare of any sails, but now the masts were strung with rigging and great grey sails filled with the wind and billowed out into the night sky. The ship heaved up and back down and a wave crashed onto its bow and over the side to his right swirling across the deck and passed him.

"This can't be happening." He said to himself. But David was close up behind him looking over his shoulder.

"No it can't be," said David, "but it is."

The ship heaved again. In the darkness through the rain William saw the silhouette of a figure. It stood beyond the main mast at a large ships wheel. It seemed the figure was struggling to hold the wheel turning it one way and then the other. William shouted out but the wind snatched his voice and whisked it away before his words had gone a couple of meters.

"Come on!" William shouted at David pointing to the figure. "We've got to get to him."

He set out across the deck David following behind without question. They held on to whatever they could as they staggered over the deck to the figure at the wheel. As they neared it William shouted again. This time the figure heard him. It turned to them as they came close. They stopped a couple of meters in front of it.

A man faced them stubbornly still holding on to the swivelling wheel. He wore a uniform. It was a dark blue with gold braid on it. His eyes were as wild as his black wavy hair, gleaming even in the darkness. He smiled at them. All but one of his teeth were white, a single one was gold.

"To the lifeboats!" He cried. "To the lifeboats! The ship cannot be saved! Save yourselves, get to the lifeboats!"

William stared at the man, his heart in his mouth.

"You're the general manager!" He shouted.

"The Captain Sir! The Captain! You address the captain of this vessel! Captain John Guy! Do as you are ordered. Take to the lifeboats. Save yourselves!"

The Captain turned away from them and again grappled with the wheel. The deck lurched.

"We've got to get back to the others!" shouted David. "The ship must be in danger! Sinking! We must do what he says!"

"Let's go back!" agreed William shouting over the wind. "But we can't leave here, this can't be real."

"But if the ship goes down!" protested David.

William was already moving back to the dining room entrance. David obediently followed him.

There was a huge thud and jolt as a massive wave hit the side of the vessel. Its water rose high above the deck and then came crashing down sweeping all before it, clearing the deck and whatever had been upon it.

The sound and the jolt of the wave was heard and felt in the dining room. Water seeped through the bottom of the door and cascaded down the stairs. Several of them screamed. Patricia held her hands together and began a prayer.

"What's happened to David and William?" demanded Barbara.

"I'll go and see." John assured her.

"We'll all go." Said Robert. "We can't stay here. We've got to leave, get off this thing."

"We can't, we can't!" protested Barbara.

"We must!" said John and Robert together.

"We can't stay here. We mustn't stay here." John added. "Come on! All of you!"

They helped and held on to each other as the ship lurched from side to side. They made it to the stairs and struggled up them. John opened the door. They saw the scene that had greeted William and David.

The Captain was no longer at the wheel. He was coming across the deck towards them. The group came onto the deck but stayed by the door. The Captain stopped a few paces in front of them.

"To the lifeboats! To the Life boats!" he cried. "The ship cannot be saved! Save yourselves, get to the lifeboats!"

Robert spoke up. "Where are our friends? Have you seen them? What's happened to them?"

"They have gone." The Captain told them. "Now, save yourselves! To the lifeboats, follow me!"

He turned and without thinking or arguing they followed.

Again a great juddering shook the ship from port to starboard. Each of the group reached out for anything they could lay their hands on to steady themselves. The deck rose and lurched to the starboard. It hung for a moment as if in mid air. Even the wind seemed to abate and for a second an eerie silence fell. And then the ship fell, sank back into a trough of water. On the port side a great dark blue-black wave loomed above them. It too seemed to hang there for a second. Screams rent the air and as they did so everything moved. The wave crashed upon the deck. The ship lurched to starboard. Deep cold sea water surged across the deck. It tore at the hold covers, smashed against the great wheel, and it beat against and broke open the dining room door. And with it as it swept across the deck and back into the sea it took the debris it had created, it took everything that had not been securely fastened, and it took whoever was upon it; save but one.

The events manager had sat at his desk. He remembered that the clock was close to midnight. He dozed off and awoke suddenly when the clock was approaching 2am.

It was late. He had to get the party to leave so he went briskly to the ships dining room. There was no-one there. They had already left. It saved him the job of getting them out, but he was dismayed at the state in which they had left the place. Chairs were upturned, glasses of wine were knocked over and staining the white tablecloths, candles and their holders on the floor. It was more like the scene of a stag party than a middle aged class reunion.

He would leave it as it was until the morning. He wouldn't let the cleaners start on it before he had shown it to the general manager. They would want compensation for this.

In the morning the general manager looked at the devastation. His eyes gleamed. He nodded and said. "Don't worry they won't be coming here again."

The police were bemused. They had never had to pull ten bodies out of the dock in one go before. The DI had established that they had all been partying on the ship the night before and, most certainly, had been drinking heavily. Although the weather was bad and the dockside slippery and dangerous it seemed very peculiar that all the people could have fallen into the water and drowned. But all the evidence pointed to that. Whatever other explanation could there be?

The Dowager's House

The Dowager still liked to be known as such. Whether she was or was not a real Dowager, some said a Dowager Countess, was not known. But she had once owned the house known as the Dowager's House and so the name had stuck. It had stuck to her mostly because of her insistence upon it. She never had letters addressed to her as such, as the postman had noted, but some had been addressed to her as 'the right honourable' Mrs Orton so there was probably a direct link to a title at sometime in the past. Some people thought that it had come to her through marriage to a man believed to be a Viscount. The story was that he had died not long after their wedding and after the traumatic event she had become a recluse.

The house she inherited, The Dowager's House as it became known, was a large sprawling residence set high on a hill overlooking a number of acres of grassland that led steeply down it. The hilltop where the house stood was well wooded on three sides but open to view on one side over grass hill. It was a prominent structure which had in years past been painted a highly visible orange colour. And, since the construction of a motorway at the base of the hill, had become a notable local landmark.

For a short time directly after her husband's death to cover the properties high running costs she had rented it to the local authority which used it as a mental hospital. But times changed and such establishments were closed in favour of more modern medical methods. It has to be said that the rumours of the time regarding the poor treatment of the inmates became the subject of a full scale inquiry in later years with those affected and their families demanding reparation.

Mrs Orton was left with alone in the building. She lived in a small part of it that she could barely afford to keep heated in the winter. Without proper care and attention, year by year, the house fell into disrepair. Mrs Orton was left in an empty and decaying property.

It took many months but eventually her solicitors and financial adviser persuaded her to sell the building and its land. However she put some quite stringent provisos upon the sale.

Her first demand was that. Although the land went with the house, no further buildings were to be erected for the next one hundred years. Her second was that she be afforded free accommodation in a small part of the house, which she would specify in advance, for as long as she lived and, more strangely, that upon her death these apartment were to be sealed and never used again.

Despite her solicitor's efforts, knowing that it would make the sale much more difficult, Mrs Orton would not budge, she would rather die with the house falling down around her. So the solicitor gave way.

Surprisingly they found a buyer quite easily who was keen to convert the property into apartments and accepted Mrs Orton's provisos without hesitation.

It had taken Anna Iveson several months to find somewhere she could rent at the right price and availability. The problem she kept encountering was that whenever she found a place she liked and that she could afford someone always else always beat her to it, she never seemed to be the first in the queue. Then her luck changed.

It wasn't quite the ideal place as far as transport was concerned and its proximity to shops but she fell in love with the location immediately. The small but perfectly arranged one bed-roomed flat was in a large converted house – The Dowager's House it was called – with a fantastic view from a hilltop overlooking both the countryside and the city. It was only the motorway at the bottom of the hill and the continual low drone of the traffic that spoiled it somewhat.

But she said yes to the agent right away and, having drawn the deposit from the bank in advance, handed it over and secured it for herself there and then.

Her flat was on the ground floor at the western end of the house. The lounge looked out over the hill and her bedroom was on the western end overlooking the trees. The flat next to hers also looked out over the hill and took up the rest of the western half of the ground floor. It was the Dowager's apartment.

Anna walked past the door to the Dowager's rooms every day. Anna had lived there for three months and summer was turning to autumn and the trees outside her bedroom window and around the grassy hillside were becoming burnished in shades of copper. In all that time she had never once spoken to or seen the Dowager. Although, as Anna left early for work and often came home late in the evening it was not entirely surprising that she did not encounter her during the week but she had thought that she would have done so at the weekends. But the Dowager never made an appearance, at least not when Anna was present in the corridor. She knew, however, that the Dowager was there as she could on occasion hear noises through the wall that separated her lounge with a room of the Dowager. Often it sounded like people talking, sometimes music. Anna assumed the old lady was watching television or listening to the radio.

Neither had she seen any evidence of her neighbour from the outside. Her lounge had French windows that opened out onto the lawn and grass; the lawn being the first fifty metres of grass that the gardener had mown. In the summer Anna would often open the doors, take a blanket, and lay it and herself out on the lawn in the sunshine. From that position she could easily see the windows and French doors of the Dowager's flat. But the view into the room was always clocked by thick net curtains and almost closed full length curtains behind them.

It was clear to Anna that the Dowager was a recluse but she often wondered how she got her shopping. The dowager would have to buy food. Perhaps she did so during the weekdays when Anna was at work. Perhaps the Dowager did not go anywhere but had what she needed delivered. It was a small mystery that recurrently came to Anna's mind.

Anna had taken a day off work, she had a dental appointment in the afternoon, had some holidays to use up so had taken the whole day. She was sat in her lounge having a mug of tea and was reading a book. She had not bothered to turn on the radio or TV and was sitting in a peaceful silence. She began to hear what seemed to be an argument coming from behind the Dowager's wall. It sounded as if it was a radio play that the old woman was listening to. The volume of it rose. The Dowager must have turned the sound up; perhaps she was hard of hearing. The sound distracted Anna for her book. She could not concentrate on it and had to put it down.

The argument was between a man and a woman, or sounded so to Anna. After a while it faded away. Anna couldn't help but walk to the wall and listen. There was no sound of any music or anything else that might be the end of a radio program or the start of another.

A loud thud hit the wall. It made Anna jump back from it. Voices were raised again and sounded louder or closer to the wall. It was mostly the man's voice. As his voice trailed off Anna thought the heard the crying or sobbing of a woman. Then those sound too died away.

Anna was worried. She no longer thought it was a radio or TV. She was sure it must be an argument between the Dowager and some visitor. She wondered what to do. It had not sounded as if anything terrible had happened but clearly the woman was very upset and the thump against the wall had felt violent.

After some thinking Anna decided to knock on the Dowager's door to make sure she was OK.

She left her flat and went to the Dowager's door. She waited outside for a moment listening, still wondering if she should knock. All was quiet. She had raised her hand ready to knock on the door. She brought it down almost deciding not to knock after all, not to interfere. What should she say? Should she just introduce herself after all this time living here? That might seem odd. Should she mention hearing the argument? That might not be the most tactful approach. Perhaps if she just mentioned hearing the loud thud? She could just say that she was worried that the Dowager had fallen and hurt herself and wanted to make sure she was all right.

That was the approach she would take. She raised her hand again and knocked on the door. She waited. She listened. There was no sound. She leaned a little closer to the door and raised her hand to knock again.

Silently and surprisingly the door opened. Not too far, but enough for the Dowager's face to be seen.

Her face was thin and lined, her hair was grey and held in a bun at the back. She was the same height as Anna. Her eyes were a dark blue. Anna could see that she used make-up in an old fashioned way; her face was powdered and a blush of rouge was on her cheeks. She must have used a small amount of eye-liner and mascara. It was the mascara that Anna could see had run and then been hastily wiped away. But the sign of her tears were still there.

"Oh, hello." Said Anna nervously and backing away from the door slightly. "I'm sorry to disturb you, I heard a bang, I was worried you might have fallen and hurt yourself, that you'd had an accident."

The Dowager stared at her.

"Oh, I'm sorry, I'm Anna, I live in the flat next to you. I don't think we've been introduced before."

The Dowager straightened herself but the door remained as it was.

"I know who you are." She told Anna in a precise and what Anna would have called a rather posh accent. "I know who everybody is. It is my house you know. I wouldn't have anyone living here if I didn't know who you were."

"Um, no, well, I just thought I'd introduce myself and make sure you were Ok."

"I am perfectly fine thank you." the Dowager told her and cocking her head to one side.

"I see, well, if there's anything I can do. If there's anything you need, just let me know. Don't be afraid to ask."

The Dowager cocked her head to the other side. "Afraid? What would I have to be afraid of?"

"I just meant, don't worry about calling on me at any time."

"I see. Well, that is kind of you."

The Dowager just stared at Anna. Anna felt uncomfortable.

"Well." said Anna, "I'll just get along then. Remember, anytime." She turned and walked to her door.

"Anytime?" the Dowager asked.

"Uh, yes, anytime."

"Thank you my dear, Miss Iveson, I shall remember that."

Anna turned in time to see the Dowager's door close and she retreated to her flat.

'Miss Iveson.' Thought Anna, 'She called me Miss Iveson, I hadn't told her that. But she did say she knew all about the people living there. I imagine the agents told her who was moving in. And there was no sign that there was anyone else in her flat, unless they were hiding in the background.'

By then it was time to make her way to the dentist.

It was getting dark when she returned; the nights were really drawing in. She hesitated at the Dowager's door. She didn't know why and had to shake herself before continuing on to her own. As she put the key in the lock she heard a noise. She looked back. It had come from the Dowager's flat. Was it another argument, raised voices? She listened. Then there was another sound but Anna couldn't work out what it was but it certainly came from the Dowager's flat. Anna retraced her steps and stopped before the Dowager's door, held her breath and listened.

Anna started. The door had suddenly opened; she had barely seen it move. The Dowager stood there.

"Oh, I thought I ..." began Anna. "You're all right then." She didn't know what to say. She had been caught eavesdropping, caught unawares.

"Is there anything I can do for you?" asked the Dowager.

"Um, no, I'm sorry. I shouldn't have.... shouldn't have stopped here."

"That is perfectly all right Miss Iveson." The Dowager smiled.

"I'm sorry, that's twice today I've disturbed you."

"Oh, you didn't disturb me this time Miss Iveson."

"Anna, please call me Anna." Anna smiled and held out her hand.

The Dowager looked around the door and along the corridor. It was deserted. She took Anna's hand and held it for a moment. The Dowager's hand was cold. She looked into Anna's eyes and then smiled and took her hand away.

"Well, as you are here, Anna, why don't you come in for a moment?"

"Well, I don't want to..."

"Not at all, not at all. It will be a pleasure. I don't have any young company these days."

"Well, for a short while perhaps. I've some things to do before going to work in the morning."

"Come in, come in." The Dowager welcomed her as she opened the door wider.

Anna entered the Dowager's apartment.

The curtains were drawn as they always seemed to be from the outside. Several wall lights provided the only illumination. The furniture was not just old but old and expensive, antique furniture. Old paintings were hung on the walls which could have adorned any large country house or even a museum. Anna glanced around. She could see no radio or TV.

"Please take a seat." Said the Dowager pointing to a particular one.

Anna thanked her and sat.

"I had just put the kettle on for a pot of tea, I'm sure you would like to join me. And some biscuits perhaps; Bourbon are my favourites."

"Yes, that would be lovely." Anna smiled.

The Dowager left the lounge through the door to what was the kitchen. Anna was sat facing it. The layout was a mirror image of Anna's flat. She took another look around. No radio, no TV or any other electronic device that any usual flat would have these days, not even a telephone that Anna could see.

She heard a noise from the kitchen. She listened intently. It was not the sound of a boiling kettle. It was certainly a voice. Perhaps the old lady talked to herself, it would not be surprising living alone like this.

She heard a noise coming from the kitchen. She listened intently. It was not the sound of a boiling kettle. It was certainly a voice. Perhaps the old lady talked to herself, living alone like this it was hardly surprising.

Anna tried to pick out the voice. Was it the Dowager's? It must be. Anna was tempted to get up and sneak over to the kitchen door to hear better. But she had just been caught doing that outside. How embarrassing would it be to be caught at it again? She forced herself to remain seated and strained to hear the sounds from the kitchen.

There was the noise of cups and saucers, the clattering of teaspoons. That must have been what the noise was.

But then, once more, voices, definitely voices. And this time Anna was sure that she could hear two. One was certainly a woman, the Dowager, the other sounded like a man.

'What if,' thought Anna, 'this was like that old film Psycho. The Dowager playing the two parts herself. Maybe playing herself and that of her dead husband. People did that sort of thing when they got older. Or when they were ill; mentally ill.

Now Anna felt ill at ease. She would have the tea and then quickly leave.

The kitchen door opened and the Dowager emerged with a large silver tray on which were a teapot, cups and saucers, and a plate of biscuits.

Anna smiled at her and the Dowager smiled back. The kitchen door closed. Anna glanced at it. Again she thought something was odd. How had the Dowager opened the door with the large tray in her hands, and how had it shut without her assistance? Maybe it had just swung shut. But the sense of unease returned.

"There, my dear," said the Dowager as she placed the tray on an oak coffee table in front of Anna and taking the seat opposite her, " tea and biscuits."

She poured the tea into the two cups.

"Milk?" She asked.

"Please."

"Help yourself to sugar."

"Thank you."

"Now my dear Miss Iveson, you must tell me all about yourself."

Anna hesitated but as the Dowager smiled sweetly at her she began and told her of her life from beginning to end. Nit that it was much to tell. She had a pleasant childhood but both her parents had died recently and she was now alone. She was an only child and had no cousins that she knew of. Her private life was almost as solitary. Just a few close friends and currently no boyfriend.

"I know how you feel my dear. I have been all alone since my husband passed on. He was only young. But I manage to draw strength to keep going. Somehow I find a way."

"Well," said Anna putting her cup in the tray, "I'd better get going."

As she spoke there was a sudden noise from the kitchen as if some crockery had fallen from a shelf or off a work surface. It startled Anna who stared at the door.

The Dowager's face went blank for a second and then she brightened. "Oh dear," she said, "that must be Mr Guy."

Anna looked back at her. "Mr ....?"

"My cat." Explained the Dowager. "Mr Guy. I named him so."

"Oh I see. Well I'd better be getting along." Anna said as she stood, thinking, 'That must be who she speaks to.'

"Of course my dear. Mustn't keep you. It has been such a pleasure to have you here. I would love our little friendship to continue."

Anna smiled and walked to the main door. "Of course, I'll try and come again as soon as I can."

Her back was turned to the Dowager. She turned the door handle. It was tiff. She tried again. No, it wasn't stiff, it didn't open, it was locked. She turned.

"The door seems to be ..." She stopped mid sentence. The old lady was nit in her seat. The tray was still on the coffee table. Nothing else had changed.

"Hello? Where are you? I need to get out."

Anna looked over at the kitchen door. The old lady must have gone there to see to her cat and what it had done.

She walked to the kitchen door and knocked on it.

"Hello. Are you there? Please, I need to get out, the door's locked."

There was no answer. No sound from the kitchen.

Anna grabbed the door handle and turned it. The door opened. She looked into the kitchen.

It was surprisingly modern, unlike the lounge. It was very clean and tidy, nothing seemed out of place. But there was no-one there, and no sign of a cat. What there was, was another open door. It was older than the other fixtures. Anna wondered if it was a pantry. She called out again but there was no response. She walked over to the open door.

Steps led down from it. It was quite dark and poorly lit. It led to a cellar. Perhaps the Dowager had gone down there searching for her cat. Anna called out once more but still got no reply.

Reluctantly she began to descend the stairs.

She could put her hands out to each side and feel the walls and use them to steady her descent. The steps were old and worn and turned gradually to the left. They were lit by some widely spaced and rather dim lights.

She reached the bottom. A room stretched out ahead of her and two more to the left and right, but it was difficult to see into them because of the gloom. She called out again for the Dowager. The reply was silence.

She walked forward a few steps calling out again and then a few steps more. The walls were damp as was the floor, and the air was cold.

She shivered, she didn't want to stay down there.

There was a bang. Anna jumped. Her heart leapt into her mouth. It was suddenly darker. She looked back the way she had come. There was no light coming from where the steps should be. She went back the way she had come, it was only a matter of a dozen paces. She reached a wall. The steps should have been there, she was sure the steps should have been there. She felt panic rising in her. She must have veered off course. She would follow the wall around to the right, she was bound to find the steps.

The dim light flickered.

Anna stopped.

The lights went out.

Anna let out a whimpering scream. She almost ran around the wall feeling it as she went. There were no steps. And then her hands felt air and not wall. She stumbled about, her arms held out in front of her. She screamed for help.

She stopped. She sobbed.

She took a deep breath and tried to compose herself. She tried to think. But she was in blackness, literally and in her mind.

Anna heard a sound. It was like footsteps, like the padding of feet. She held her breath. She looked around in the darkness but it was almost impossible to see anything. But then she saw lights. Relief surged through her. Lights, lights to the steps.

There were two of them. They glowed, but they were not lights. Two eyes glowed in the darkness.

Anna screamed. The eyes close on her. She could see around them what looked like the glossy shine of black hair. She tried to scream again but no sound came from her throat. She was rigid in fear. She could sense the smell of something odd, strange, a peculiar mixture of lavender and rotten meat. It made her want to throw up. She felt the brush of hair, or was it fur, against her and the heat of breath upon her neck.

There was a knock at the door. It opened. The Dowager looked out from the gap to see who it was.

"Good morning madam." Said the man.

He was holding out his identification for her to see.

"Detective Constable Harris madam; I wonder if I could ask you a few questions?"

"Well, certainly Detective Constable."

"It's about your neighbour next door, Miss Iveson. Have you seen her recently? Or heard or seen anything unusual?"

"Why, no. In fact we have never met. I keep very much to myself you know. I've never even seen her, just heard he come and go."

"And have you heard anything recently?"

The Dowager thought for a moment. I can't say I have, not for a couple of days or so anyway. I expect she's gone away somewhere."

"And you've not heard anything unusual at all?"

Nothing Detective Constable Is there something wrong?"

"Just making enquiries madam, she'd not been seen for a few days, not turned up for work."

"Oh dear. I hope nothing's happened to her."

"Let's hope not. But thanks for your help."

"Not at all young man, happy to oblige."

He passed her a card with his name and telephone number on it.

"If you think of anything here's my contact details."

"Oh my, they give you business cards these days, how professional!"

"All you have to do is call the number and I'll come over."

"Will you really? Oh well, I'm sure if I think of anything I'll be calling you."

The door closed and the Dowager vanished.

DC Harris walked a few steps and then stopped to write up the interview in his notebook. He heard a noise from behind the old lady's door. It sounded like raised voices. He listened. It seemed to be the voices of a woman and a man.

The Mansio

Paul scraped away at the hard earth with the trowel. Today he had remembered to bring a cushion to kneel on. Yesterday he hadn't. It had been a tough long day. He couldn't kneel properly, the ground was dry and felt as hard as concrete, and uneven concrete with stoned and pebbles jutting out through the earth and biting into his knees. He had tried to just sit on his haunches but that was as bad on his back as kneeling was on his knees. And so he had ended the long hot summer's day with both pitted, grazed knees and a painful back.

Today was easier. There had been a shower or two overnight and the ground had softened. He was working in a corner of the grid in which the mosaic floor was being uncovered. There was only his part to clear before the full floor was uncovered. A small scaffold tower had been erected beside it to take photographs from above. Each time he scraped and uncovered more mosaic he was still amazed at how bright and clear the colours were. The floor, covered for nearly two thousand years, looking as pristine as the day it was last trod by sandaled feet.

The site was that of a Roman Mansio; a Mansio not a Mansion. A Mansio was much like a modern day Motel, it was an inn and resting place with rooms and a bath house where travellers could relax. It was close to a Roman road and there would have been a continual stream of officials, messengers, officials and soldiers passing along it wanting a place to rest.

The archaeologist in charge of his section wanted the floor uncovered as quickly as possible but not to the point of neglecting any other finds. Subjected to the air for the first time in all those years the colours would fade. He wanted to capture the whole of the mosaic floor in its most colourful state before that happened.

It was almost at the point of the last scrape of the trowel that Paul saw the glint of metal. His trowel had scraped over an object lying on the mosaic floor, and it was a bright metal. He had previous uncovered the odd Roman coin and small iron artefact but he had not seen anything gleam as brightly as this before. He needed to call the supervising archaeologist over. This would have to be carefully uncovered and removed. It would also hold up the final clearing of the floor.

He stood and looked around for his supervisor. There was no-one near him, and no-one in authority anywhere that he could see; only a few volunteers like himself at the opposite corner of the site.

He stood with his hands on his hips and stretched his back. The archaeologists must all be at a meeting, or more likely a long tea break. He supposed he would have to go over to the finds tent and try and find one of them.

He looked down at the glinting metal, the rays of the bright sun touching it and reflecting from it after all those years in darkness. He looked around again but there were still only the few distant volunteers. Perhaps he could just dig a little around it with the tip of his trowel to see what it might be; or perhaps not.

He bent down to take another close look. He put his trowel down on the ground beside him and took a closer look. All he could see was a circle of metal embedded in the earth. It looked like silver but it was completely untarnished; perhaps it was gold. By instinct he took out his phone, lined up the camera, and took a picture.

He reached down to touch it. The metal tingled in the tips of his fingers. He couldn't help but brush some of the earth from it with those fingers. The trowel remained on the ground unused. It was a large circular object, larger than a ring. It was more the size of his wrist. He looked up from where he crouched; still no-one about apart from the volunteers. Surely if he was careful, just brushing the earth away with his fingers, no harm would be done. And he could take pictures as he did so.

The metal seemed to shine both as silver and gold. Could it be a mixture of the two; he'd never heard of it before. He touched it again. The tingling feeling returned to his fingers. It gave off some sort of power, electricity almost. Maybe the light of the sun touching it for the first time in millennia had an effect on it. This time Paul felt the tingling and a warmth running through his arm and his body. The glow from the object filled his vision. He could not help himself; he reached down and scraped away more of the earth with his fingers.

Now he could see the entire thing. It was a bracelet or amulet of some sort. His fingers reached around it and gently pulled. There was no resistance, it lifted from the earth. He brushed away the dirt that still stick to it with his other hand. It fell away as easily as if the surface was a modern non-stick one. He stared at the bracelet; he could not take his eyes from it.

Around its outer surface was an intricate repeating pattern. It was not like anything he had seen before; not that he had seen much before. Certainly it did not look Roman. But it was lying directly upon the Roman mosaic floor so could not have been from any other period.

The world around him was silent. He was in his own world now. He could not resist the temptation of the bracelet, for temptation was what it exuded. What was, and what happened around him, was no longer of any importance. It was the bracelet that held all that was important; it was the bracelet that filled Paul's mind, an irresistibility that he could not ward off or deny.

And so, without a thought, he pushed his right hand through the bracelet. It was a tight squeeze but his hand went through. And then the bracelet hung upon his wrist.

Paul smelled a strange smell. His nose wrinkled. He still stared at the bracelet on his wrist but now the world around him that had been silent was coming to life again. From the emptiness that had encompassed him before, save that of the bracelet, the world around him was once again filling the void.

He was kneeling on the same mosaic floor. It was bright and it was colourful and seemed more so than it had been before. He tore his eyes away from the bracelet and looked around.

There were walls, walls around the mosaic floor, and in the walls small windows. Above him was a roof of timbers and stone tiles. Around the room were couches and in the corner on a table stood a container from which a curl of white smoke rose, an incense burner and the reason for the smell.

He stood. His mind was still somewhat blank from the experience of the bracelet. This must be a dream; he must have fallen asleep in the sun. He pinched himself. The pinch felt normal but this could not be normal. Where was he? How had he got here? The last thing he remembered was being on the dig, on the mosaic floor.

He looked at the floor and the pattern on it. He knew it, he knew it very well, and it was imprinted on his memory. He had been staring at it for days. But now he stood, not in the open upon it, but inside where it had been two thousand years earlier.

Once more he looked at the bangle. It fitted snugly to his wrist, very snugly. It now fitted his wrist perfectly and there was no give, no looseness to it. He tried to move it but it slid along his wrist only slightly. He doubted he could now get it over his hand to take it off.

He sighed. It worried him.

But what worried him more was where he was. He knew in his heart where he was and, even if he didn't want to, in his mind. He knew it was the

Mansio. And he also realised, and inwardly knew, it was not really a matter of where but of when.

He couldn't just stand there in the middle of the room. He had to find out the truth of it. He must look outside the room.

He could see the wooden door and headed for it. The bright sunlight bathed the room as he opened it. He passed through and out into it.

He turned around and looked at where he was. The room he'd been in was at the end of a large building, a complete building, the Mansio. Smoke rose from a chimney at the other end. That would be the fire for the hypocaust, the under-floor heating used in the colder weather. It would also heat the water for the bath house and would also be used as an oven for baking bread and cooking meals.

He could hear horses. The sound came from behind the main building. He knew that was where the stables would be. In front of the Mansio there was cleared ground and, passing by, the Roman road. Beyond it was woodland where there should have been open fields.

He now sure of the where of it and also the when, but he had no idea of the how. The what was what to do about it, and for that, for now, he had no answer.

There was nothing for it but to take a look around.

The sounds of people and activity came from the Mansio, beyond a veranda and where there was a communal area. Paul made for it.

Several people stood around a man and a horse. A couple of them were poorly and basically dressed, obviously workers or even salves. Another man was dressed plainly but of better quality cloth that had a pattern around its edges and he had good leather sandals upon his feet; probably the Mansio's owner. Standing by the horse was, without any doubt, a Roman soldier, probably though Paul a centurion.

The slaves and the Mansio's owner noticed him. They fell silent and stared. The centurion followed their gazes and turned to look at him.

Paul realised he must have looked very odd to them. All he could think of doing was walk slowly towards them, stop and hold his hand up palm outwards in a sign of peace and, what he thought, was a Roman sign of welcome; he'd seen it in films.

It was the Mansio's owner who spoke first. But that was of no use to Paul. He may have been on a Roman archaeological dig and had a real interest in Roman history, but he knew very little Latin, in fact almost none. This was going to be difficult.

The centurion held up his hand to silence the owner and apparently to take charge as the most senior person there. He passed his horse's reigns, which he had been holding, to the owner then took a few steps towards Paul. Paul felt his heart thump and his throat dry.

The Centurion was tall, taller than anyone else there. His eyes were a dark blue-black. He wore no helmet and his black wavy hair shone in the sunlight. The centurion smiled at Paul and a single gold tooth sparkled in that light.

The Centurion spoke. Paul's head swam. The bracelet gave him a tingling sensation that spread up his arm. He found it hard to focus. He was getting double vision, two Centurions stood before him. The voice of the Centurion echoed in his head, a jumble of unrecognised sounds.

The, slowly, his mind began to clear, his vision steadied, two of each thing merged back into one. His breath, which had become erratic, eased to normality.

The voice of the Centurion continued to speak to him.

But now Paul could understand him.

"So, you are the one." said the Centurion. "You have come."

Paul blinked. He looked at the man hearing him but not understanding.

"I have waited for you. I was about to give up."

"I can understand you. I can understand what you are saying." Paul said incredulously.

"My speech may not be that of a true Roman but I speak it as well as the next man. And I am a Roman."

"Who are you?"

"I am Centurion Guido of the 1st Hispanorum of the Petriana Alae. But that is not of so much consequence. I was sent by another to greet you."

"To greet me? How could you know I'd be here? I shouldn't be here anyway. I don't know how I got here."

The Centurion, Guido, looked down at Paul's wrist and spoke. "But you wear the bracelet."

"That?" said Paul looking at it and touching it. "I found it. I put it on. I know I shouldn't have, but I did." He paused. "And then I was here. I should never have put it on!"

"You did not choose it, it chose you. And now you are here as prophesised."

"I want to go back! Please help me, help me get it off, cut it off even!"

Guido gave him a steady, icy stare. His face darkened and he glowered at Paul. "That cannot be done. What is, is, what has been, has been. And what will be, will be."

Guido turned away from him. "Come." He said. He started walking away from Paul towards the door the main room of the Mansio which acted as a lounge, bar and eating place. Automatically and silently Paul followed him.

They walked through the room. It was difficult to see much having come indoors from the bright sunlight. Guido opened another door and Paul followed him into a small ante-room.

In the room was a small altar, a lararium Paul remembered they were called. Guido had immediately begun taking off his cloak and breastplate and underneath it a vest of chain mail and placed them in a corner of the room from where he picked up a white garment, a clean cloak or shawl. His sword still hung by his side.

"What are you doing?" Paul asked warily.

"We must give thanks to the gods." Guido told him and turned to the small altar on which there were several small effigies and carved idols or representations of gods. In the middle a small copper saucer contained some already burning incense. To the side was another dish of Samian pottery that Paul recognised and a small silver knife along with a slim glass flask; accoutrements for whatever religious practices the believers of these small gods engaged in.

Guido checked that the door was shut.

That unnerved Paul somewhat. He didn't like the feeling of being trapped in the room.

Guido went to the altar.

"Come," he said, "join me."

"It's all right, I'll just watch from here." Paul quickly said.

Guido turned, his eyes seemed to shine and bore into him.

"You must join me. It will not take long. There is nothing to fear."

Paul swallowed hard but could not resist the stare. "Ok." He said meekly taking the few steps to join Guido at the later.

"Stand beside me." Guido told him, and Paul complied.

Guido picked up the small silver knife; another action that made Paul shiver.

It was then Paul first noticed the band around Guido's wrist; a silver band, a bracelet. He looked at the decoration on it, then at his own. It was the same as his, a duplicate.

Guido noticed his look. "Yes, they are one and the same." He said staring into Paul's eyes. Paul was becoming mesmerised by them. He could see nothing else; his vision was filled with Guido's face and, most especially, his hypnotic eyes.

"We are brothers." Guido added. "At least we will be so. We are destined to be; brothers in blood, as one."

Guido took hold of Paul's arm, the one which he wore the bracelet. Paul was unable to stop him, to counter what Guido was doing. His feet were of clay. If he could move he would have done. If he could have run to the door and escaped through it he would not have hesitated. But, under Guido's constraining gaze, he could not.

Guido brought up the knife between their gaze. The silver of it glinted.

"We will be blood brothers." said Guido. "Do not worry it will not hurt, it will only be a scratch. Just a small drop of blood is all it will take; a drop from you, a drop from me, the two joining each other in brotherhood."

Paul was gripped by paralysis, not able to move of his own volition, not able to speak of his own will.

The knife went down to their forearms, each forearm clasped with the bracelets.

Guido first put the blade to his own arm. He drew against the skin. A line of red, oozing blood appeared next to the bracelet.

The knife moved to Paul's arm. Paul's fearful eyes watched it. Again it drew a line. The line on Paul's arm drew blood.

Guido took his arm and Paul's and held them close together, one on the other, blood upon blood, bracelet upon bracelet.

Paul felt the same tingling he had felt before, coming from the bracelet and flossing up his arm. But this time it was slightly different, it was harsher, it was more of a stabbing, a pain. He opened his mouth to scream. But, of course, he could not. His vision began to blur. A mist started to surround what he saw. Guido's face, his shining eyes, became enveloped in the mist. Paul felt his breathing becoming more shallow and fading and as it did do the white mist was also fading but being replaced by a deep darkness. The darkness turned to black as his breathing ceased.

-:-

The supervisor asked the volunteers if he had seen Paul. He had been working on the final part of the mosaic floor but the supervisor could not see him there. No, they said, they had not seen him.

The supervisor went over to where Paul had been working. His trowel was still lying on the ground next to where he worked. What was odd was that alongside it was Paul's mobile phone. Perhaps he had an urgent call and had to leave. But surely he would have told someone. And why would he have left his phone behind? It was most peculiar. The supervisor picked up the phone and trowel and took them to the finds tent; Paul would be able to pick them up the next day. Meanwhile someone else would have to be found to finish off the work on the mosaic.

Paul didn't return the next day for his phone. But the police arrived. They wanted to know when and where Paul had last been seen. The supervisor told them and handed over Paul's phone.

The dog carried on for several days. Paul did not return. But the police did. They had his phone. They had gone through the calls, texts, and data. They had a question for the supervisor. There was a photo of a silver object partly in the ground. They wanted to know where it had been taken, what it was and what had happened to it.

The supervisor was perplexed. The date time stamp of the photo would indicate that it was taken just before Paul had vanished, but no such find had ever made its way to the finds tent.

The police asked if it was likely to be valuable and were told that, yes, it probably would be, but its value in terms of knowledge would be greater than any monetary value.

Perhaps, the police suggested, Paul had stolen it and run off.

Three more days passed.

The dig was uncovering a small room at the opposite end of the site. The supervisor was called over by some excited volunteers. Someone had made an important discovery. On the floor of the small room by the side of some small idols lay a skeleton, the complete skeleton of a young man. Around the bones of his wrist was a silver bracelet, a bracelet the supervisor had seen before.

Captured On Film

He had not expected to have ended up working as a librarian. He had trained in aerial surveying, photographic surveys of the land in order to make and update maps. And not just surveys relating to this country but also of countries abroad whose governments paid for the work to be done, or for whom it was done virtually free of charge as a gift which gave this country a bit more diplomatic clout. The job could have meant travel abroad. If not, it at least gave the work in producing maps an added interest, an opportunity to see foreign lands from a perspective that no ordinary traveller ever would. But besides the highly technical task of producing maps it was also their job to manage the library of films.

But here he was working as a librarian, an archivist of all the many aerial films that had been accumulated over the years of both here and abroad.

It was still a valuable source of information. Comparative reports of the changes to the land over the years and to the growth of towns and cities provided vital information for academics and government organisations. And so the old films, as well as the new, were in almost constant use by various departments and agencies.

He had thought that the work would have been confined to the normal working week, nine to five, Monday to Friday. But no, it seemed that requests came in at all hours from the rather less than public departments when there was some crisis or other in some obscure part of the world; or for that matter in a very less obscure part. And so a duty librarian was required to man the library at night and deal with the requests. Most nights were quiet and boring with almost nothing to do but read a book and wait for the phone to ring. And once midnight came they were able to sleep in a side room that had been set up with a bed.

The library was big, racks upon racks of shelving filled with large tins of film mostly nine inches tall and of varying widths depending upon the length of film inside. It was on two levels with a long wide aisle down the centre with row upon row of racks either side. To optimise the space the racks were on rails. There were some eight racks on each rail but the only space between them was the width of one rack; the racks had to be pulled apart on the rails to get to the rack that had the shelf that held the tin of film that the librarian required.

A usual trick upon a newcomer was to send them to a particular location then, when they were in the space between the racks collecting their tin of film, sneaking up and pushing the rails together to trap the person vice-like in between the racks, then scooting quietly away. When the person extracted themselves the perpetrators would be safely back in the office working at their desks and denying any knowledge of it. The racks were known to have a mind of their own at times. They could, it was said, sometimes move without human assistance. One could often hear sounds of the racks moving and creaking even if the place was empty; but everyone accepted that it must just be the racks settling into position some time after being moved. Sometimes the lights would flicker and even go out leaving a librarian in blackness and no-one admitting to having touched a single light switch. But someone must have, mustn't they. It must have all been designed to frighten a new recruit to the job.

The one thing that no-one could ever quite explain and which unnerved even the longest serving member of the library staff was the voice. It was very rarely heard. But, one by one, over a long period of time, one librarian or another would swear to have heard it. And for some time afterward would not go into the library alone. The story was told that it was the ghost of the first librarian to have worked there. He had gone missing, disappeared into thin air. He was never found, never discovered. It was his soul that stalked the racks of film.

Perhaps it was only heard at a particular time when the wind blew in a certain direction, when the racks were in a particular position, when the settling of them upon the rails and the odd tin of film moved a little against the metal of a shelf and created a voice-like sound. Perhaps that was all it was.

And it was the one thing that a duty librarian staying behind alone at night was always conscious of.

Another department would receive the requests for photographic cover. They would do a computer search of a database and request the film that gave the best coverage. Normally someone would bring the printer paper request along in person.

This particular night had been very quiet. Danny, for that was his name, had spent most of the evening reading a book and making cups of tea.

He decided he had stayed awake long enough and prepared to take to the bed, firstly going to the toilet. When he came out of the toilet he took a final look around the office. On the floor was a sheet of paper. It must have fallen from one of the desks. He picked it up. It was a request for a film. Someone must have tried to deliver it when he was in the toilet. He had locked the door, as was required, so they would not have been able to get in. Not willing to wait they must have slipped it under the door. On the top of the paperwork was indicated its priority; it was urgent.

He sighed and got to work. He checked the reference number of the film requested and went to his computer screen. The library database had not yet been integrated with the coverage database. Danny, as well as everyone else, thought it was long overdue. The librarians would not have to do a separate search to find the film's location it would be already printed on the request form.

He logged on and entered the film's reference number.

Its information came up on the screen. He noted the rack and shelf number on the request form. The history of the film's use also showed on the screen. It had only been used once before, and a long time ago. In fact the date of withdrawal and return was the same and must have been when the library had first come into use after its move from a previous location.

Danny wondered what part of the country or world it covered. One would know where if the coordinates had been noted on the library data. In this case they had not. Another way to tell was by the film's reference number. Sometimes it was not just a number but also a set of letters. They could be a clue.

In this case he noticed that the letters GUY were part of the reference. Perhaps this indicated a country; Guyana maybe. He had not realised they had any film of the South American country, but as it was a British colony at one time it was possible. He wondered what was so important or urgent to request the film at this time of night.

The library was in darkness. He had kept the lights switched off but now switched them all on. Light bathed the length of the library; bright along the aisle, but darker further back into the racks either side.

Danny looked down the long aisle and then at the printout he'd taken. The film was at the very far end on a corner rack. It was where some of the oldest films were located. He sighed again. The he began his walk towards it.

He reached the far end and checked the location. The films position was on a bottom shelf of the furthest rack on his right. He went through the gap between the two rows that separated the line of racks. He had to push apart all of the racks upon their tracks that had enclosed the final one, the one he had to get to. They were heavy and he moved first one half of them and then the other. The final rack was now accessible. The shelf was the furthest one at the bottom fitting snugly into the very corner of the building.

He went to it and bent down. The shelf was packed tightly with tins of film of different sizes. All of them looked very old and much of the writing on them had begun to fade. With his luck, he thought, he'd have to empty the whole shelf before he came across the one he was looking for.

One by one he took out the tins, checked the reference numbers and placed them on the floor beside him. Dust had settled on each of them over the years and wafted up with the movement they had probably not felt in all that time. It made him sneeze.

He had to bend right down on his hands and knees to get to the final few tins. None had the correct reference number until only one remained pushed tightly into the very farthest corner. He stretched out his arm, gripped it in his hand, and retrieved it.

GUY was on it, the reference number checked out. This was the one. But he couldn't leave all the other tins on the floor; he'd have to put them back before returning to the office.

The lights dimmed. At least to him they seemed to dim. He stood up holding the tin in one hand and the paperwork in the other.

Now the lights seemed to be normal. It must have been the effect of being on his hands and knees in the relative dark.

He bent down again and began replacing the tins keeping the selected one to his side. He put the last of them back on the shelf. Again the lights seemed to dim.

He got up. He was sure that it was not as bright as it had been although the lights nearest him glowed as they should do. Maybe one of the strip-lights nearby had gone out.

He heard a noise.

He listened. He held his breath and listened.

Nothing; it must have been the settling of the racks that he had just moved.

He bent down again to pick up the tin of film. He held it in his hand. Besides the reference number it had the shelf location written on it in paint rather than the permanent marker that was later used, and was old enough not to have any bar code. The library was still undergoing the process of adding bar codes but only when tins were withdrawn or returned without them. That would mean another job for Danny to do in the office; he'd have to print out a bar code and stick it on the tin.

It also had a date on it; the date that the film was taken, that of the aerial sortie. But in this case there must have been a mistake. The year had to be wrong. No-one was flying aerial surveys, yet alone flying much at all, in 1901. Someone was having a little joke. It wasn't uncommon.

He looked at his printout. The date was the same on that. It should have been rejected on input but clearly someone had found a way to bypass the check and added to the lark; clever, but it would mean he would also have to sort that out as well.

The lights dimmed again; this time significantly so. Above him the strip-lights glowed but nowhere near as brightly as they should have. A power cut maybe. The backup generators would have come on but not powerfully enough to keep the lights fully on.

There was a noise again; like a whispering.

It was close to him. But it could not be. He was alone. He was the only one here.

There it was again. It must be the wind outside. It blew across the surrounding farmland and sometimes whistled through the steel fence and barbed wire that surrounded the building. Perhaps it was the wind that had brought down a power cable.

He must get back to the office. If the lights failed he would have to feel his way back in blackness.

"Wait."

It was not a whisper, it was a voice.

Danny's heart almost stopped and then thumped rapidly. He pressed his back up against the rack. He held his breath. He listened and waited. Was that not the word of command?

He shook his head to clear it. He was letting the light and the wind get to him. Now he was imagining voices. He must get back to the office.

"Help me."

It was a voice, not a whisper. It was not the wind. It must be in his mind, in his imagination. But he had not moved he was stock-still, almost rigid, backed up against the rack.

As fear rises do does the adrenalin and as it does the automatic response to run, to get to safety, imposes itself upon the body.

"No. Don't go!"

It was louder this time. Loud enough to dent the body its response and safety catch.

Danny had all but stopped breathing.

His eyes slowly looked down to the tin he held in his hands, This was some terrible trick of some sort. The tin had been rigged. Something in it, a small tape machine perhaps, set to start up when the tin was moved, set to frighten anyone who picked it up.

"No trick. Help me."

Danny stared wide-eyed at the tin. There was no mistaking that the sound had come from it. He wanted to put it down, put it back on the shelf, say he had not been able to find it, leave it for someone else to find, in the morning perhaps.

He swallowed hard, stared, waited and tried to think what to do.

It was a trick. He was absolutely sure of it. He swallowed again and tried to relax his muscles. He could open it up. He'd take out the device and show everyone in the morning.

He put his hand on the lid. He heard what he thought was a sigh, one of pleasure, one of both relief and intense satisfaction.

He hesitated. He could hear the wind outside whistling through the fence and around the building. There was a storm brewing. Maybe it was just the wind.

He turned the lid and pulled.

At first it was stiff; then suddenly it gave and came away.

The lights went out.

There was blackness.

There was the sound of the wind from outside and a musty breeze inside along with a deep sigh of relief.

Danny had been holding the tin but he could no longer fell it in his right hand or the lid in his left.

The feeling at his back was solid, not that of the racks and the shelves.

He shouted out. Whoever he had heard must be close to him. But there was no sound. It was silent. There was not even the sound of the wind outside. He called again; he called for help. Nothing.

The blackness around him was truly black.

He put his arms out in front of him. He needed to feel the racks, make his way between them, walk as a blind man down the aisle, feel his way to safety.

His arms did not go far in front of him before he felt something; a solid surface. He felt with both hands. He followed the surface. It was not flat, it was curved. He felt around the curve, and around, and around. It was as if he was in a large circular pipe. The surface of it was cold. It was metal.

A black gloved hand reached down to the tin and picked it up. Carefully it placed the tin back on the shelf. And quietly the racks were drawn together again.

It was a long time since the first librarian had been so free. But now Mr Guy's chains had been broken and he was at liberty again.

The Man on the Bench

In all the years that they had lost contact Terry had always wondered what had happened to Mick. Forty years had passed. It seemed like a lifetime away, in fact in some countries of the world it would be just that.

Terry had visited Mick and stayed at his parent's house when they had been best friends. He remembered it well. It was in Bournemouth. He had been to Bournemouth a number of times since then, just for a few days at a time, for a long weekend staying at an economical bed and breakfast or, more recently since he'd retired and was a little more comfortably off, at a hotel. Even then he always tried to get the best deal possible using a last minute booking site.

Each time he'd visited he had thought of Mick and his visit to him all those years ago and wondering what had happened to him.

When they had known each other they were both serving in the RAF. Mick was in a different trade but they had become close friends when they'd both been DJ's in the NAAFI Club. They could almost have been brothers. There may have been some people who thought they were more than that, but that would have been untrue. Mick had been married for a short time before joining up. His wife had had a child, a girl, and then they had separated shortly afterward.

The one thing that could be said about Mick was that he was something of likeable rouge. He had a continual habit of landing himself in trouble, mostly of his own making, and was often on a charge and on 'jankers'; not actually locked up for the indiscretion but forced to do some demeaning job after working hours and reporting regularly to the guardhouse in an immaculate uniform to be inspected by the duty Sergeant.

On one occasion it had led him to be given the task of cleaning the floors of the other ranks mess at night when all the work had been done and the staff had left. He would make sure the job was done properly and would pass inspection by the mess sergeant the next morning; But it also presented him with an opportunity and temptation. Attached to the kitchens were the mess stores and, to have access to the mess to do his cleaning duties, Mick was allowed to sign out the keys to the mess. The key bunch contained the keys to the stores.

It didn't take him a moment to realise that, given the right contact on the outside in the civilian world, there were items in storage that could be worth a pound or two; nothing too obvious that was regularly checked but such things as potatoes, onions and other items that were continually used in substantial amounts and resupplied on a daily basis.

Needless to say Mick's plan didn't work. The mess Sergeant, with the time coming close to his annual assessment, had decided to take a much closer interest in the comings and goings of the stock. He had made careful note of the stock levels, made his Corporal take an exact note of what was used during the day, and had personally checked the incoming supplies. It only took twenty four hours for a disparity to appear.

Nothing could be proved and no-one could be accused without proof. And so the Sergeant ensured that an extra stock check was made at the end of the day just before the mess was locked up and, as the Corporal came on duty and started his shift first thing the next morning, a further check was made.

It only took one night to discover both the culprit and the hidden pile of potatoes not far from the back door of the mess where the supplier could both unload a new delivery and relieve the mess of part of an earlier one.

Mick was charged with theft the same day.

The Commanding Officer decided that discretion was better than both giving the camp a bad name and an additional black mark on his own career in not managing a well run and respected Station as it should have been and always was. An agreement not to go to court in return for an instant dismissal on compassionate grounds was quickly made. Mick was free to go as a civilian and the Commanding officer was free of an undoubted rogue.

Terry had not heard about all of this. It had happened whilst he was on a Station skiing expedition in the Scottish Highlands. His friends were quick to update him on the details, or as many of them as they knew considering the CO had tried to keep a lid on it, as soon as he returned.

Terry only heard from Mick once more after that. Mick had put a telephone call through to where he believed Terry worked. The operator connected it to the crew room where Terry took it. Mick didn't say much. He realised when the operator gave terry's rank that he had been promoted, congratulated him and asked how he was. Terry said he was fine and asked how Mick was. Mick too said he was well, that he had found a job and was living in Bournemouth. It was a brief call and ended all too quickly.

Terry wondered afterwards why it was that Mick had called him out of the blue with apparently very little news. Perhaps he was in trouble again, perhaps he needed help. Terry was annoyed with himself for not asking enough questions. But now he was unlikely to find out; he had not even asked for a telephone number or address.

And so, forty years later, Terry still wondered what had happened to Mick.

Terry, now that he was retired, could pick and chose the best time to go on a few day's break, both in terms of cost and weather, and had logged on to his computer to search for accommodation. He found a last minute single room going at a remarkably low price at a four star hotel that overlooked the gardens, seafront and pier. He grabbed the chance and booked it immediately from a Friday night until a Monday morning. He then booked a return train ticket at another good rate.

As he completed the bookings he recalled the visit forty years before and thought about Mick. Was he still alive? Did he still live in Bournemouth? If he did what were the chances of bumping into someone there if you took time wondering the streets? Knowing his luck the chances would be pretty slim. It was odd how you could bump into the same people in a large town and city for no apparent reason against all the mathematical chances when you had no particular wish to, but how it would be impossible to have a chance encounter with someone when you really wanted to.

He had searched on line for Mick's full name before; on Facebook and on Google on the chance that something might crop up. The closest he got was a few years before when he discovered someone with the same name who'd also been in the RAF. He had sent a message to him and asked if he had served at the old Station but the person said they had never served there and had been in a completely different trade.

Terry decided to search again. More and more people were now on Facebook and more and more data was now searchable in Google. So, he typed Mick's name in again.

There was nothing new in Facebook. But when he searched on Google he added the criteria of 'Bournemouth' as well as Mick's full name. There was an instant result, both for the name and Bournemouth; well, not quite Bournemouth but Boscombe which is to all intents and purposes part of the same town.

The result was a local newspaper report.

A man had been giving evidence in the Coroner's court after the discovery of a body in a bedsit. The man had been staying in the deceased's bedsit against the rules of the tenancy. One morning he had let in another, female, acquaintance when she had rung the door bell. When she entered the lounge she screamed when she realised that their friend was a lifeless body lying on the settee.

The man who had been in court was Mick. It must have been Mick. It was not just someone of the same name from the same area but the age was exactly right. It must have been him.

Mick had denied that his friend had been dead when he had left him to open the door. But the autopsy had shown that his friend had been dead for at least twenty four hours. Mick said that they had been watching a DVD together just before he had gone to the door. As far as the Coroner, or the Police, were concerned this was impossibility.

However, the Police admitted that, by the time they had arrived at the scene Mick had been heavily intoxicated and had probably been so for some time beforehand, so much so that he would not have remembered anything that had happened for a number of hours previously. Tests on the body also revealed that the subject had been heavily intoxicated and to the extent that it had caused the man's death.

No blame for the death was placed upon Mick as the Coroner and the Police both believed that the cause of death was natural and that Mick had not reported it earlier as he was too drunk to do so.

The odd thing was that Mick continued to deny he had been drinking heavily or that he was drunk and that his friend had been alive just moments before he had gone to the door. But the case was dismissed.

Terry had three weeks to wait before his trip to Bournemouth. He had decided to become a bit of a detective and try and contact Mick if he was still in the area, which he was sure he would be.

So, meanwhile he searched for other clues. Nothing else turned up. Until, that is, he was looking on Google street view of the street in Boscombe where the bedsit had been. He saw nothing so extended the search to include the main street of the town. It would also give him an idea of the place before he visited. He usually did that to have a look at the hotel he'd booked and the surrounding area to see what it was like and to check out the surrounding bars and restaurants.

It was as he was looking around the main street that his attention was taken by a man sat on a bench. Google had become expert at hiding the very things that we'd all like to see especially if you wanted to be an investigator, like the numbers of houses, car number plates, and people's faces. Terry carefully changed his position on the street to get as many different angles as possible and as detailed one as possible of the man on the bench. They were all faceless. All but one. On one view the man's face had not been pixelated, it was quite clear, especially once he had zoomed in.

It was Mick, Terry was absolutely sure of it. And the bench was at a junction only a short distance from the reported address. It was Mick and he must still be in the area.

But by the look of him he was not in a good way. It looked as if the years, his life, and the recent court case had taken its toll. In fact he looked like he may be homeless, someone who may well have taken to the bottle, someone who may have been as drunk that fateful day as the police had suspected.

Three weeks went by and Terry was on his way to Bournemouth. Not too long a journey but long enough with a change of train at Southampton. He arrived at the hotel an hour earlier than the booking in time and had a drink in the bar waiting for his room to be ready. Once he got to his room and settled in it was the afternoon and he decided to leave going to Boscombe until the next morning. He would spend the rest of the afternoon and evening strolling around Bournemouth.

Wherever he went he could not help but take notice of any single elderly man sitting on a bench. Any one of them might be Mick. And one became many. There were more people sitting on benches looking as if they had no home or whose lives depended upon just another drink than he would have thought. It was easy in everyday life to walk on by and not notice them. But when your mind is concentrated upon such a person, when your eyes are open looking for such a person, they are not hidden from you; you are aware.

The next morning Terry ate breakfast, checked the bus times and walked to the bus stop from where he could take the short journey to Boscombe. The buses were many and regular and he was there in a short time.

He got off the bus at one end of the main shopping street. It was a long wide and pedestrianised. To him it looked more substantial than Bournemouth shopping centre which was split into two by the River Bourne and central gardens. The stop where he'd dismounted was at the other end of the shopping centre to where he had seen the man on the bench and the address where Mick had been. The weather was fair, sunny and quite warm and he strolled along the street looking at the shops but also keeping an eye out for anyone who looked like Mick, especially older man sitting on any of the many benches that placed along his path.

Once again he was surprised at the number of men who might have fitted Mick's description. He was tempted to stop and talk to one or two of them but none looked quite like the man he had seen on the bench and so he kept going towards the end of the high street and the bench where he believed he'd seen Mick.

He came close to the end of the high street where the road of traffic which had bypassed the pedestrianised area rejoined it and all became traffic again. On the opposite side of the junction was the bench. It was empty. Terry considered what to do. The address in the newspaper report was only a couple of streets away so he decided that, for now, he would walk along it and back again in the very slim chance of bumping into Mick; that is of course, if he was still in the area.

He went to the road, walked up it one way, then back down again. It was a tree lined road of substantial houses none of them looking as if they contained bedsits for the less well off. He bumped into no-one yet alone Mick.

He returned to the junction. The bench was till empty. He hung around the nearby shops and looked into their windows whilst still keeping an eye on the bench. First a woman with a pram stopped and sat there, Then a couple of teenagers who rolled and smoked a cigarette or something similar, and then the bench was empty again. It was getting near lunchtime so terry decided to walk back down the shopping street and taking a look again at anyone on any other of the benches. Then he'd grab a sandwich for lunch and sit on one himself.

He got his lunch after he had walked back along the full length of the shopping street. There were some benches just in a side street away from the shoppers. He decided to eat his sandwich there. The bench was already occupied by an old man, too old, short and plump to be Mick, and with a mop of white hair and a large white beard which, come December, would have made him a great Father Christmas.

The old man had a half bottle of dark rum in a bag by his side and he was only too willing to talk even though it was simply to berate someone who had befriended him and stolen all his money; so he said. Terry told him Mick's name and asked if he knew of him or heard of him, perhaps he had seen him on the bench at the other end of town. But he said he hadn't. The old man began to ramble telling him stories of the war. Terry decided it was best to move before becoming too familiar and finding it cost him to listen to the old man's stories.

He started looking again from where he had got off the bus. Twice more he sat on a bench next to a likely suspect. This time they clutch bottles of strong cider or lager rather than strong spirits, but the effect would be the same. Each time he managed to enter a conversation, albeit affect by the amount of alcohol they had already drunk. Luckily it was still relatively early in the day so they were still relatively intelligible. He was careful and wary about doing so but each time they seemed only too willing to have someone to talk to. Neither had heard of Mick, or said they hadn't, and neither could give much useful information between drifting off into stories of their own significance. But one did briefly mention that there was a nearby Salvation Army Church and hostel. Maybe they could help.

Terry made his way there.

The Salvation Army don't give out information about their 'residents' but Terry was allowed to write Mick's name on a piece of paper with his own name and contact number should Mick be one of their residents or should turn up there.

It was now mid afternoon. Terry decided to take one more walk up the high street to the bench. As it came into view he saw there was a single man sat on it.

Terry came to a stop. He watched the man rolling a cigarette. The man both looked and was dressed like the man Terry had seen on street view. He had the same features and was about the same height as Mick. He wore the same clothes as on street view. Terry wanted to get a better view. He strolled over to a shop window directly opposite the junction and the bench. He could see the man's reflection in the pane of glass, Terry was sure it must be Mick. Terry turned. He made the decision. He walked, more purposefully this time, to cross the road and get to the bench.

He waited with two other people for the traffic to ease and allow them to cross. He kept an eye on Mick. In his mind he now called him Mick; his mind had been made up that it was him.

He crossed the road. He casually approached the bench then sat on it a couple of feet away from Mick.

Terry looked at Mick.

"Do you mind?" he asked.

Mick had just lit a roll-up. He blew out a cloud of grey-blue smoke and turned.

"No." said Mick.

Their eyes locked. Both had blue eyes, Mick's lighter and more intense than Terry's. It is not easy to forget someone's eyes if you've been close. Terry knew it was Mick.

Mick's face had a blank look as they both stared. Then his eyes narrowed as if a wisp of smoke from his roll-up had got into them. And, if it had been the smoke, became watery, perhaps a prelude to a tear or two.

"Mick?" Terry asked.

Mick's body slackened and he let out a smokeless breath.

"It's me; Terry."

Mick shook his head, negatively. "Why?" he asked. "What are you doing here?"

"I wanted to find you." Terry explained. "It's been a long time."

Again Mick shook his head. "You shouldn't have done."

"It's been forty years. You were my best friend. I wanted to know what had happened to you, know if you were ok."

"How? How did you find me?" Mick asked, looking almost frightened.

"A newspaper report. I saw it on the internet."

"Oh, that."

"Yes. The address it gave is just up the road from here."

Mick stared at him. "But you found me here." He said looking from left to right seemingly checking out the area. "I try to keep off the streets mostly."

"I wouldn't have known you were here but I saw a photo, well a shot on Google street view. You were on it, sat here on the bench."

Mick's eyes narrowed. He dropped the cigarette on the ground. "A picture? Of me? Here?"

Mick appeared almost frightened.

"It was just one shot, that's all, just one shot where they hadn't pixelated your face, that's how I knew."

"You found it." Said Mick looking shocked. "Anyone could find it."

"Calm down. It's Ok. It was just a bit of luck. I don't think anyone else would find it unless they were looking especially hard and were very lucky."

"I must go. I can't come back here. He'll find me."

"Who? What do you mean? Who'll find you? Is someone after you?"

Mick stood. "I have to go."

"Let's go to a cafe or somewhere, let me buy you a meal, a drink, or something. You can tell me what's going on. What you are worried about."

Mick gave Terry a stare before making a decision.

"We must get away from here. There's a cafe up the road. We'll go there. Quickly."

He turned and walked away. Terry jumped up and followed him.

They got to the cafe. They said no more other than ordering an all day breakfast and mugs of tea. Mick made sure they took a table at the back of the cafe well away from the window but sat so that he could keep an eye on it and the door.

They didn't say anything as Mick wolfed down his meal. Terry hardly touched his, he'd already eaten, and when Mick had finished his plate he passed his over to him to polish it off as well. It was as if Mick had not eaten for days.

"So," said Terry at last, "who's looking for you, what's it all about?"

Mick wiped his mouth with the back of his hand and took a mouthful of tea.

"The man who killed Trevor." He said.

"Trevor?"

"You said you saw the story?"

"You mean your friend who died the one in the bedsit?"

"Yes, Trevor."

Terry recalled the story and that Mick had insisted his friend had not been drunk when he'd died. "But it said that he was drunk. He probably died from alcoholic poisoning."

"They said he was drunk. They said I was drunk. But we weren't, neither of us. Trevor didn't just die he was killed, murdered."

Terry found himself begin to feel sorry for Mick. The drink had probably got to him and he was imagining things, imagining things differently to what actually happened, perhaps as some sort of defence mechanism, hiding from reality, hiding from the truth.

"But," said Terry, "they did test didn't they? There was a lot of alcohol in his body."

Mick looked at him, his eyes showing some sparks of anger.

"You don't believe me. Just like the others. Why should anyone believe me?"

Terry talked calmly. "Tell me everything, exactly what happened. I promise I'll believe you."

Mick looked doubtfully at him. He hesitated. But then he relaxed little and said, "OK. If you promise."

"I promise."

And so, speaking quietly, Mick told his story.

Trevor was lucky to find such a nice bedsit in that neighbourhood. And it was cheap. Neither of them had a job so had to live on benefits. Trevor let him stay there. It was against the rules but as long as they weren't caught out what did it matter? Mick admitted they both drank, sometimes heavily, but only when they had just got there benefits, once the cash had gone they couldn't afford it. And they had run out of cash and weren't drinking when it happened.

The landlord was a strange man. Mick hadn't seen him but Trevor had told him that he was weird. Trevor couldn't put his finger on anything exactly, it was just the way he spoke and the way he looked at you. Trevor thought he must be foreign, he had an odd accent. Trevor had always shivered when he'd spoken about Mr Guy the landlord.

The day it all happened Mick had been at Trevor's bedsit as usual. They had just begun to watch a DVD. There was a knock at the door. It was Mr Guy. He told Trevor he was coming in and pushed his way through the door. Trevor tried to stop him. The landlord was supposed to give twenty four hours notice if he wanted to check anything in the bedsit, or he had to be invited in. But Mr Guy was a big strong man and he easily forced his way past Trevor.

When Mr Guy saw Mick there he lost his temper. No other person was supposed to be in the bedsit, he'd said. Trevor tried to say that Mick was just a visitor. Mr Guy was frightening; he frightened them both just with his presence and his look. Mr Guy didn't scream and shout when he lost his temper, it was different. It was a sort of calm but ferocious anger that neither of them had seen before. He told Trevor he would pay for it, pay for breaking the rules. Even if it meant with his life. And he shouted at Mick, he told him that he'd get him as well, that one day he would come for him.

Mick found it very difficult to explain what happened next.

It was as if the world changed, as if they were no longer in the bedsit, or not the bedsit as it was. It was like another place and yet the same.

That was when everything went misty and dark. Mick believed he fainted.

When he woke it must have been several later, at least the DVD that had only just begun when Mr Guy arrived had now come to the end.

Mick was lying on the floor. Trevor was lying on the settee.

Mick called the police.

They didn't believe anything he said of course, and Mr Guy denied having been there at all. Yes, they said they found a huge amount of alcohol in Trevor's body and a lot in his own, but he swore that neither of them had been drinking. And would swear it to this day. What he did know was that Mr Guy was lying, he had been there.

Somehow Mr Guy had made them unconscious and had got alcohol into their bodies. It had killed Trevor, Mr Guy had killed Trevor.

He had lived but he lived now remembering the words of Mr Guy, the words that he would find him and come for him. And Mick knew what that would mean; he knew that he would be next, that Mr Guy would kill him as well.

Terry had found him easily enough, so could Mr Guy.

Terry didn't know what to say. He had promised to believe him and he must at least show him that he did. But, more than likely, it was a vision of some kind brought on by alcohol. He had no doubt that both Mick and Trevor were alcoholics. Mick's mind had somehow created a story to cope with the fact that alcohol had killed his friend. And his subconscious was telling him that the demon drink would come for him next. Terry must try and help him.

"OK, well, as you say, it might be dangerous for you to stay around here. You need to find somewhere else to live. Let me try and help you."

Mick was shaking his head. "no, you mustn't get involved. He'll only come for you as well. Once he's come for me."

"I'm sure no-one will come for me just because I'm helping you."

"No, you're wrong, he'll come for you as well, it's best you leave here, leave me alone. I'll get away from here. He won't find me."

Terry sighed. "Look, don't do anything immediately. Let me meet you again tomorrow. We can have another chat, something to eat, talk things through."

Mick became very calm and sat looking at Terry for a few seconds.

"OK," he said, "meet me at the bench tomorrow morning. But now you'd better leave. Don't be seen with me."

Terry nodded agreement. "All right." He stood up. "Tomorrow morning. You promise?"

Mick nodded. "I promise."

Promises are kept and promises are broken.

Terry kept to his promise. He went to the bench the next day, his last in Bournemouth. He waited. He waited all morning. But Mick did not keep his promise, or was unable to. Terry walked to and fro along the streets, passing the bench, throughout the afternoon. He visited the cafe where they'd eaten and Mick had told his story. But Mick did not appear.

Terry returned to his hotel somewhat sad and disappointed. What would happen now to Mick? Terry could guess, but it wasn't a happy thought.

The next day he returned home. He had at least seen Mick, met him, talked to him and tried to help him. But perhaps he should have tried harder. Now it was too late and he regretted it.

Terry was at home on his computer. He had not kept a screen shot of Mick sitting on the bench so he went back to the street view to do so. He felt he should keep a photo of him and would print off a screen shot as a keepsake. He didn't have a single photo of him when they'd been friends. He could have taken one when they met up but it didn't seem appropriate in the circumstances.

He zoomed down to street level. He found the junction and could see the man on the bench. He had to get to exactly the right shot that had the unpixelated view.

He found it.

He looked at the man on the bench. It was odd; it didn't look like Mick, not like the shot he had seen before. He zoomed in closer. He took a good at the man on the bench. It wasn't Mick it was someone else.

It was a well dressed man in a dark suit and coat. He was obviously tall, taller than Mick and had black wavy hair. The man's eyes were sharp and alive and stared at the camera lens, stared at it and through it.

Terry zoomed in a final step closer.

The man's eyes held the camera's lens in their gaze and through it held Terry's eyes in a hypnotising grip

As the man stared through the screen he smiled. The man smiled at Terry. It was an evil smile.

Taken Into Care

Robert looked out of the wide panoramic windows at the scenery beyond. The entire side of the room was glass. The light poured into the room so that during daylight hours the room lights were never needed. The walls as well as the ceiling were painted white and the room glowed from them in the reflected light. Even the soft carpeting was near-white as well as the chair he always sat in. The room was bright, almost too bright; bright in a way that was not necessarily warm. There was a coldness to the ceaseless white and the lack of colour in any furnishings. In fact there was a lack of furnishings or ornamentation.

Robert had no idea what it may look like in the dark, whether or not the moon and the stars still shone in the sky, whether the room itself was in light or in darkness. He was only ever here when it was light, never when it was dark.

There were others here of course. He had no idea how many. But he knew a few of them, the nearest to his left and his right, they too in their chairs looking out of the great glass window and the world beyond. To his left were Holly and Mille and to his right Charles and Toby, everyone beyond them was out of earshot. Charles was the oldest, he said he had been born in 1932, then it was Robert and Holly who had both come into the world three years later, then Millie and Toby who were the furthest from him and who also had contact with those beyond. Charles talked to him the most, sometimes too much, sometimes when Robert would prefer just to sit and stare, and usually it would be of something pointless or trifling.

Robert liked to think. He thought about things a great deal. He had always been a thinker, some would say a dreamer. Even at school he would stare out of the window during lessons daydreaming they said, thinking, he believed.

And he thought about this existence. He thought about the endless days and the endless routine of sitting and staring, or sitting and thinking in his case, and the world here, and the world in the bright sunlight outside the panoramic window.

And he tried to think about how long he had been here, tried to remember. Several times he had tried to count the days as they passed, but then he had lost count and had to start again, and then he would forget the number he had reached and finally, instead of starting again, he had given up. He wished he had not given up. He could not remember now how many days his counting had reached, but it was a lot. And even that day of forgetting seemed a long time ago.

Now and then a visitor had come to talk to him, one of his family he imagined. What he did remember was that when he first came here he would regularly get a visitor coming to talk, but he now found it difficult to remember the last time someone came to talk. It was, he thought, as long ago as the day of forgetting. That was then and this was now. And now it was mostly Charles who talked to him; for what that was worth.

There was a faint recollection of his first day here. He had not been well. He needed treatment and care. His family, he was sure it was his family - if he remembered correctly he had a son and a daughter – who had decided that this was the place for him. That thought was still held somewhere in his memory. But how or when he had come he could not remember.

He began to imagine that this place was not a real place; that it was an imaginary place, that it didn't really exist, that it was, in a sense, only one of his daydreams. He imagined and wished that the endless succession of days here need not be. He imagined that, by changing the daydream, the reality of his existence could also be changed, that he might even roam beyond the glass into the outside world. He would be able to smell the air, the plants and flowers, hear the sounds of birds, feel the breeze upon his cheeks. If he imagined his daydream clearly enough, if he believed in it strongly enough, if his mind accepted it easily enough, then that would be enough. It would be enough for his daydream to become reality.

And so he sat and dreamed. He let his thoughts go free, roam to where ever they wished, allowed them to create another world. He fell into a trance-like state.

He saw a place that was not like the one he had known. It sparked a memory in him. He had seen something like it before. It was a long time ago, a very long time ago, a lifetime perhaps. But it was not an actual place, it was an imaginary place. Not a place from his imagination but of someone else's. He tried to understand it. It was a world of light and dark, of coloured patterns that moved and grew and touched one upon the other, and of brighter sparks of light streaking along the patterned lines at phenomenal speeds. It reminded him of that which was imagined in an old film he'd seen.

He tried to concentrate, to delve into his memories and discover which it had been. What film had he been reminded of? He dug out the memory. He had been getting old when he had seen the film. It was about computers and a man who entered them, and in them he fought a battle like the games that his grandson had played. Yes, he remembered that as well now, he had a grandson. His imagination had brought him into a dream world such as that.

He listened. He could hear sounds now; voices. They were garbled, mixed up, indistinct. He struggled to pick out one voice from another. He forced himself to make out and individual voice and its words against what was becoming a louder cacophony of sound.

He heard Charles. Charles was speaking, saying something. Charles must be talking to him, breaking into his daydream. No, it wasn't Robert he was talking to it was himself. Thought after thought was coming out as a stream of words.

And the other voices; Robert began to make more of them out. There was Toby, Holly and there was Millie. All of them, not talking to him, but articulating their thoughts as words.

Robert didn't like his daydream any more, he wanted to wake from it, and he wanted to be back in his chair in the room looking out of the window.

He opened his eyes. There was the window. There was the outside and the sun shining through. He breathed a sigh of relief. He relaxed.

But with nothing to do but to think he began to think again.

He thought about the world he'd created in his dream. Was it just an echo of the memory of that film he'd seen so long ago? It had felt so real. It had not felt like the dreams he used to have; which made him think. How long ago had he dreamed? How long ago had he last dreamt? He knew you that didn't always remember your dreams; only very rarely. But even though you didn't remember them in detail you always knew that you had dreamt. He couldn't remember the last time he'd had that feeling. And the more he thought of it the more difficult it was to remember when he had last truly slept, when he could recall being fully asleep. Perhaps you didn't as you got older. Perhaps your mind just switched off for periods of time without you even realising. But surely you should remember lying in bed waiting to fall asleep, sometimes lying awake not able to sleep? He couldn't recall the last time lying on bed awake waiting to sleep.

Was this heaven? He thought to himself. That would at least answer some questions. He had never been particularly religious, never really believed in God especially as he got older and, most of all, did not believe in a place called heaven.

This place must be what he believed it to be; he was in a care home, he was being looked after in the remaining days of his life. His family had put him here and, after time, had all but forgotten him.

But his daydream kept coming back to him as well as the memory of that film, of the man inside the computer, of his existence there, outside of, but still connected to the real world. If such a thing could be done would a man know which world he was in? The man in the film knew because he had been told, it was part of his knowledge and his memories. If it was not, how would he know?

Robert looked over at Charles and wondered what he was thinking.

"What are you thinking?" He asked.

Charles' eyes flickered into life. "Uh, Eh? What?" He turned his head to look at Robert. "Did you say something?"

"I said, what are you thinking?"

Charles grimaced. "Nothing." He said. "Not thinking of anything."

"We're always thinking of something, all of us." Robert told him. "You just can't remember that's all."

"Don't think I was thinking anything much."

"I heard you."

Charles frowned. "Did I speak? Sorry I don't remember. What did I say?"

"You didn't speak. I heard you thinking."

Charles stared at him. "You've been here too long. Perhaps I should call the nurse."

Robert smiled. 'Perhaps we've all been here too long.' He thought.

He settled back into his chair and closed his eyes. Again he let his mind and thoughts go free. One more he entered his trance.

He was there again. This time he looked very carefully at everything, taking his time. He heard the voices. He was about to cast them aside, filter them out, but decided to let them stay. He watched the sparks of light racing to and fro. He wondered if he could move within the place; take himself from one place to another.

He focussed his mind. He would try to capture a spark of light with it and be one with it, and to go where it went. His mind concentrated on a single point on one of the coloured grids. Several sparks went passed. His mind was unable to join with them. He tried harder. A spark came. His mind grabbed it.

The sensation was astonishing. They speed was so great that all around him was a blur. Almost as soon as his mind had grabbed it he let it go.

He was in the same place but different. The patterns were different but the landscape was the same.

But the voices were different.

-:-

"There's an anomaly in core 56." Said the technician.

"I'll take a look." Said the Manager.

The Manager was drinking a cup of water at the dispenser. He finished it off and walked to his workstation. He tapped at a few keys and clicked on his mouse.

"So there is." He said. "Put the system into standby mode and we'll check it against the last backup. When was that done?"

"0600 hours. Setting up standby procedures. I'll let you know when we're ready."

"Thanks."

-:-

The voices faded away. No more sparks of light flew. The coloured grid dimmed. Robert was worried. What was happening?"

-:-

The phone rang. The manager answered it. He listened and said 'yes Sir' a number of times before putting it down.

"Just our luck, visitors. The boss is showing some families the facility. He'll be in here in a few minutes. Get everything back on line. We'll sort it out later. It can hardly be all that important."

-:-

The grid lit up again, the sparks flew and the voices resumed their chatter. Robert was relieved. But where was he now? Could he get back to where he should be? Surely if he just woke up, stopped the daydream, he would be back in the room where he should be?

But he wasn't daydreaming was he? He knew this wasn't just a dream. All he could do was wake up and see what happened.

The grids, lights and voices faded. He was somewhere else, somewhere different.

-:-

The 'boss' entered followed by several couples. Two were a man and a woman, the third two men. He was dressed in an Italian suit, white shirt and blue tie. His shoes shone like patent leather. He was tall and well built. His hair was black and wavy, his eyes blue-black and piercing. He had a quick smile and often used it, one pleasant and comforting for the clients, another for his staff, cold and threatening.

The manager hoped there was nothing on the screens that might give away any problems such as the anomaly.

The 'boss,' Mr Guy, smiled his first smile and spoke to the couples.

"This is our control room. You can rest assured that our data cores are held securely in isolation to any outside connections other than at the times I mentioned when you will be able to connect securely to our system and talk freely for the prescribed periods, depending on your type on contract, to your beloved one. It is here that their memories are kept safe and secure, that their very essence is, in effect, kept alive. Here they may live a pain free and comfortable existence for as long as you wish, or as long as the contract provides for. In effect, as long as you wish to keep your loved one's memories alive they will be alive. The download into the system is seamless and painless. The beneficiary transcends from one existence to another and need not be aware of any change in their circumstance. We find it is usually better and less traumatic for it to be done that way.

And, as far as costs are concerned, how much cheaper it is than having to pay for a physical existence in one of those old fashioned care homes, many of which no longer have the capacity to care properly for their clients. We offer you care for your loved ones without the worry of physical distress and at a fraction of the cost. And with their memories downloaded into our system neither you, nor they, will have to look forward to the loss of mental abilities. They will be as you remember them for as long as you wish to support them.

Now, perhaps we should see the download facility."

-:-

Robert heard the voices. In front of him was a window, a small window on another world, not the panoramic one with a landscape bathed in sunlight. This was a small world. It was an office.

There were people in the office, two in the foreground and others standing by an open door. It was the man in front of those others who was talking, whose voice he heard. Robert listened to him, listened carefully. He heard what the man said and began to understand his words. And the understanding of the words jelled in Robert's mind, and the understanding of his world was defined by them. They told him what he had become to believe and feared.

-:-

As Mr Guy turned to escort his visitors from the room his eyes settled upon one of the computer screens. His face changed. It paled. His eyes narrowed and a fire burnt in them. He turned briefly to his guests and regained smiled number one.

"If you wait outside I'll be with you in just a moment."

He closed the door.

He glared at the computer screen. By that time the manager and technician had also turned to it.

The large screen was a patchwork of windows showing various data streams and graphs. But in the top left hand corner was a window that held no data, what it held was the face of a man. It peered out at them.

Robert saw the faces turn to look at him. They seemed shocked and angry. The farthest of them looked particularly angry. They looked at him as adults would look have done when he was a small boy and been caught in the act of doing something terrible. It hardly took a moment for him to realise he was in trouble.

"What the hell is that?" demanded Mr Guy.

Neither the manager nor the technician said anything.

"I want that data file deleted, and I want it deleted now! I want a thorough investigation. Whatever virus it is I want it destroyed! Every data file must be checked. Any file that has been corrupted must be deleted. Do it now!"

With that he turned and left the room.

The manager looked at the technician and the technician at him.

"Well, you heard him." said the manager.

"But they are ..." began the technician.

"They are data files. And one of them has been corrupted. We must do what he said."

The technician looked at him wide-eyed for a moment and then turned back to the screen.

Robert had heard the conversation. He had not fully understood what was said but he had a good idea what they meant.

He turned to the grid. He concentrated his mind on capturing a spark of light. His mind grabbed one and he was off again. He was getting better at this. He went from that place to another.

"Shit!" said the technician as he turned to the screen. "He's gone!"

"Damn! Find him. He must have left a trace. He's in there somewhere. We can't let him infect anything else in the system."

The technician turned and looked into the manager's eyes.

"You said - him. You didn't say - it."

Tunnel Vision

"So that's it?" asked Justin.

"Yep, that's it." Matt told him.

They stood in front of a concrete box a few inches taller than either of them. One face of it, though, was not concrete, it was a solid metal door that was securely bolted and licked.

"It leads down to the tunnels." Matt added.

"Well, that's not much good is it? We can't break our way into there. Look at that door. And it's in the corner of the park, anyone could see us, and they've got cameras, over there on those poles."

"I know that." Matt sighed. "I just wanted to show you, that's all. There's other places you can get into the tunnels, it's just knowing where."

"And you know that do you?"

"I've found one of them, yes. I'll show you; but not today. I've got to borrow a Kayak from the club, then we can get into it."

"A Kayak?"

"Of course, it's down on the river, the old docks, at water level. That was the whole point of the tunnels, getting contraband goods from the old sailing ships into secret storage places."

"Yea, I know, you told me; loads of secret tunnels underneath the city going from the docks to secret cellars." Justin paused. "So, when are we doing it?"

"Tomorrow." Matt told him. "We'll get a Kayak tomorrow."

They met the next day at the sailing club where they also had kayaks. Matt had arranged for them to hire two of them for the day. On the opposite bank of what was the old harbour Georgian houses, many in assorted colours, were stacked up the hillside that fronted the docks. It was said that the old sea Captains and merchants would buy properties there so they could watch the ships retuning with the precious cargoes. To their left the harbour came to an end with a great lock after which the river took the waters to the Bristol

Channel and on to the open sea. To their right the old docks ran all the way into the centre of the city splitting up into a variety of wharf-sides.

Today the docks were the preserve of leisure craft, floating bars and restaurants and, in one or two places, some decaying commercial craft. Only one significant ship was moored there in the very dry dock where it was built and was now a tourist attraction. Even the old warehouses had been converted into restaurants, bars and clubs, together with some museums and art galleries.

Matt and Justin were dressed for their excursion and both wore the regulation life jackets. Even in what looked like the still and silent waters of the docks it could be dangerous.

Their kayaks slipped into the water and the young men climbed in and made themselves comfortable and secure. Then Matt led them to the right and towards the city centre.

Matt and Justin paddled up the docks. They passed a marina and its leisure craft, then the tall masts of the SS Great Britain with its flags fluttering in the light breeze, and passed the new elegant apartments that now occupied a stretch of the old wharf-side. Ahead they could see the dockside cranes, no longer in use but with their arms set as tributes to their industrial past, and the museum that accompanied them. And to their left was the wide concrete arc and amphitheatre of the financial services giant which now carried the mantle of the city's success.

It was at that point that the waterway split. To their left the docks went a little further to end at the city centre.

"Are we looking up there?" Justin asked.

"Far too busy. Too many people would be watching us." Matt told him. "I've had a look from the sides, there doesn't seem to be any tunnel entrances there. Mind you, at the end there's the entrance to the river that flows under the centre. It was built over years ago. Before then the docks went all the way up through the centre. You can see the huge metal grille blocking the way into that. We can't get through that even if there any tunnels ender the centre. We'll go further on, where it's a lot quieter, where nothing's been changed much for years."

They paddled on passing yet more boats, renovated dock buildings and waterside bars and restaurants.

The docks turned to their left and they followed it. Office blocks and apartments now took up most of one wharf-side. Then they paddled under a large bridge into a stretch that sided with the park where they'd looked at the concrete box, the sealed entrance to the tunnels below; or so it was said.

"There must be something along here." Matt told Justin. "It's where that entrance was."

Slowly they drifted along. The side upon which the park now stood was high above the waterline. A solid stone wall rising above them, damp, and at the lowest level, covered in green slime. Parts of it were overgrown with weeds and ivy, and water plants clogged places at its base.

It was behind some of these plants and curtain of ivy that hung from the park above that Justin spotted something.

"There!" He called. "What's that hidden behind those weeds?"

Matt stopped and paddled a little closer.

"I think that's it!" He exclaimed. "It looks like an old iron gate. It shouldn't take much to pull away those plants."

They both looked up. There was no-one looking down at them from above, they shouldn't be discovered.

Matt was right, it didn't take much to pull away the weeds.

In front of them was an old iron gate and behind it was a tunnel.

Matt reached out to touch it. The gate was encrusted with rust and slime. It only rose a metre or so above the water line but clearly went further below it.

Matt pulled on it. There was absolutely no movement.

"Here give me a hand." He said to Justin who manoeuvred over to him.

They had to get into a position facing each other so that each could get hands on to the gate. Together they pulled. Nothing.

"That's not going to budge." Said Justin. "Doesn't look like it's been open for god knows how long."

Matt sighed then said. "Hang on, don't pull, push. Perhaps it opens inwards otherwise any rush of water coming down the tunnel would have forced it open."

Justin shrugged and they both gripped the bars of the gate. They pushed. It wasn't a good Idea. As they pushed against it they pushed themselves and their kayaks away from it.

"We can't push it properly sitting in these." Said Justin.

Matt looked around. To the side of the gate was a piece of metal, like a handle, sunk into the wall.

"Mind out of the way." Matt told him. "If I get a hold on that and push it'll stop the kayak moving away."

They manoeuvred again. Matt grabbed the metal handle and pushed against the gate. There was no sign of it budging. Twice more he tried. And there was no movement.

"I's no good." Said Justin. "There's no way it's going to move. It;;s probably locked somewhere under the water."

"Yeah, I suppose you're right." Matt agreed. "We'll take a look further along, see if there's another one."

As they go their kayaks ready to move and their paddles in the water there was a noise from the gate. It was the sound of metal moving against metal or stone, a sort of clonk, as if something had given way.

They both looked at the gate.

As they looked they could both see that the gate was moving very slowly. Gradually it was swinging inward, it was opening.

"We must have done just enough to loosen something!" Matt said gleefully. "It's opening!"

Instead of paddling away they moved closer.

The gate finally swung fully open. Ahead was a dark tunnel.

Matt took off a back-pack he'd been carrying, containing what he called his essentials. From it he took two lamps that had headbands attached to them.

"There you go." He said, handing one to Justin, "put that on. They're fully charged, they'll last for ages."

They both put them around their heads and turned them on.

"After you." Said Justin, and Matt went into the tunnel.

The roof of the tunnel was only as few inches above their heads and neither of them fancied the thought of the water level rising. But for now they should be safe. The beam form Matt's lamp lit up the tunnel beyond and behind him Justin's lamp lit both him and the tunnel.

Very soon the tunnel veered to the left and then it went to the right. Matt stopped. The tunnel still went ahead but they had reached a crossroads; there were also tunnels to the left and the right.

"What do you reckon?" Matt asked Justin.

"Go back or straight on. As long as we keep going straight we won't get lost. If we start going left or tight we'll lose our way."

Matt reached into his back-pack. "I thought of that." He said, showing Justin a large piece of chalk. "We can mark our way as we go."

"Straight on." Justin insisted. "And mark our way as well."

They moved forward. As they rounded a curve the tunnel widened and the roof became higher. They entered something of a chamber. To one side of it was a ledge, a small docking place. They halted. Each of them swung their lights to and fro to examine it.

"Look, there!" Matt pointed. "It looks like a doorway."

Justin turned his light to it and agreed.

"We can tie up here and take a look. There's still some metal rings here we can tie up to." Matt explained.

Justin went along with the idea. They tied up their kayaks and got out onto the ledge or small stone platform. Matt took the lead as they carefully walked on the wet and slippery surface.

The dark doorway could now be lit by their lamps. The opening led directly to a flight of stone steps that went upward.

"It must go up into some cellars. Let's take a look." Matt said enthusiastically.

"Are you sure? What if it leads into someone's house? We'll be trespassing, breaking and entering or something."

"Don't be daft. We'll just apologise and say we got lost in the tunnels. No-one's going to get the police out for that. Come on."

And Matt began up the steps with Justin close behind.

There weren't many steps to climb before they came to a wooden door.

"Well, that's it." Justin told Matt. "We'll have to go back."

"At least let me see if it opens."

He reached out to an old iron catch, lifted it, pulled, then pushed. The door swung into whatever lay behind.

The room beyond was in light, not bright, but enough for them to see without the need for their lamps. It was lit by several old laps that looked like they used oil.

The room was a cellar with stone walls and an arched ceiling not much taller than Matt and Justin. It was being used for storage. Wooden crates lined the walls as well as full sacks and several barrels. On one of the walls was another door.

"I think we'd better get back. This is someone's cellar." Justin said nervously.

"Just a quick look."

"It's just a few old crates and stuff, nothing to look at. And it's not ours, and we're not supposed to be here!"

"For heaven's sake we're not doing any harm!"

Matt went to look at some of the crates. Justin sighed in exasperation. Matt tried to look into one of the sacks. He smelled it and frowned.

"Doesn't smell nice." He said.

There was a sound. A noise; footsteps. They came from behind the other door.

"Quick Matt! Let's go! Someone's coming."

Justin turned to leave. As he did so he saw that the door they had entered had closed. He got to it quickly.

"Matt! Come on!"

He pulled the door. It didn't move. He pulled again. Matt was behind him now. Still it didn't move. Both of them grabbed hold of it. They pulled. It refused to move, it did not open.

They heard behind the sound of the other door opening.

Both of them froze and then slowly turned to face the other door.

It opened wide and into the cellar stepped a man. He was about their height. His clothes looked strange; old fashioned. His hair was black and wavy and his eyes glinted in the light of the oil lamps. He looked at the items in the cellar and then his eyes fell upon Matt and Justin. He smiled. He had bright white teeth; all that is but one, and the gold of that one sparkled.

"Ah! There you are my lads. You've come at last. I've been waiting a new delivery. And here you are."

Justin was first to speak.

"I'm sorry Sir, we seem to have come here by mistake. We were investigating the tunnels. We can't get the door open."

"Mistake you say? No, there can be no mistake. You came by boat did you not?"

Matt spoke. "We left our kayaks down there." He said pointing at the door. "At a small landing stage."

"Kayak? A boat of some sort? As I thought, you have a boat. And what goods have you brought me?"

"Goods?" Asked Matt. "No, you don't understand. We were just investigating the tunnels. We accidently got locked in here. Can you open the door for us? Then we'll be on our way."

"No goods?" The man frowned. "You came here with no goods? No wonder the door has locked upon you." He paused. "An accident you say? You had not meant to come here?"

"No." Said Matt. "We were just looking at the tunnels that's all."

The man was silent for a moment staring at them both.

"No goods." The man repeated. "And an accident you say. But you were expected. Why else would you be here? Who else knows of this accident?"

"No-one." Said Justin. "It was just our idea. Please could you open the door. We meant no harm. We just need to get back. We won't tell anybody about this place, I promise."

"If the door will not open I cannot open it. No-one can."

"But you must be able to!" said Justin almost pleading with him.

"Not I, not that door. This door," he said pointing to the open one, "this is my door, this one I can open."

"Look," said Matt, "just help us. I'm sure the three of us will be able to open it."

The man shook his head. "Not I. That door will not open. Not without goods being delivered."

'Goods.' Though Matt. "I'll tell you what." He said opening his backpack. "I've got a few goods here. Perhaps these will do?"

"Ah! So you do have goods! But you told me you had none! Do you lie to me?"

"These are just personal things." Matt said quickly. The man looked and sounded as if he was getting angry. "It's all we've got, nothing like crates or barrels full."

He pulled out what was in the backpack. The chalk he had used, a ball of string, a bottle of spring water, some sandwiches and a spare cagoule. He placed them on one of the crates.

"There that's all we've got."

The man looked at the backpack.

Matt sighed and place that down as well.

The man walked over to the items and turned them over. He shook his head. "I do not even know most of these things. If you have no goods worthy of barter then we must find another way."

"All we need to do is get out of here." Matt tried to say calmly. If we can't go back down to the tunnel let's just leave this cellar and get out of here, that door's open."

The man looked at Matt then nodded. "Very well, many doors are open to me, but not always all of them. There are some that, one shut, will no longer open."

Matt sighed. "Well, that one's open, so let's just leave."

"If that is want you desire then follow me." The man said and turned to the door.

Matt and Justin followed his lead. They all went through the door and up narrow stone steps which curved to the right. At the top of the steps was another door which was also open. It led into a poorly lit room. Matt and Justin walked in and looked around. The man closed the door to the stairs and went over to another door which they imagined led out into the street. It was difficult to tell as the only window was covered in a thick dark curtain.

The man opened the door. Sunlight streamed in. Both Matt and Justin breathed a sigh of relief.

"Thank you." They both said together.

The man stood aside to let them out. And out into the sunshine they walked with relief.

They looked around in puzzlement. It was not like any street they had ever seen in the city.

The street was narrow and cobbled. The buildings either side rose up and over it but only by a few floors. They were made of black wooden beans and what looked like plaster. They looked like the buildings of several hundred years ago.

Along the street carts rumbled over the cobbles. Either they were pulled by men or by horses. The people were dressed in old and dirty clothes. The noise of their shouts and calls rose above the sound of the carts.

And there was the smell; the smell of the horses and of the people hardly distinguishable.

This was not the modern city it was a city of the past.

Both Matt and Justin looked at each other in horror then turned to look at the man.

He was not there. The door to the building was closed.

Matt rushed to it and started banging on it. Justin joined him. Both of them called and shouted for the man to open up.

The door did not open. It was solidly closed.

A passerby stopped. 'Ain't no good bangin' and screamin' young gents. He said with a thick accent. "Ain't bin no-one there for years. Can't remember the last time I saw any man come in nor out. You ain't gonna get no luck there." And he walked away.

A man looked over the wall from the park down onto the water below. Two kayaks floated slowly by, their paddles drifting along with them.

He took out a phone and called the emergency services, then turned away from the scene.

The two kayaks were recovered. The police discovered they had been hired from the sailing club and who had rented them. But no bodies were recovered with them, nor were they ever found.

In the park a council workman was busy replacing a big heavy lock that secured a metal door on a concrete block. Some fool had vandalised it overnight.

The police never traced the phone call that made the report. And, according to the records, no such number existed.

The Zookeeper

The tiger prowled to and fro behind the bars of his cage. He had been a big attraction at the zoo since arriving there twelve years before and was now middle aged but still in his prime. Customers had queued to walk past his cage, a metal fence keeping them just out of reach of the cage bars.

But times were changing; the idea of keeping such a magnificent cat caged in such a small space was no longer in vogue. At the end of the summer season he would be moved to a new home. He would be granted a new degree of freedom and the space to roam in a modern wildlife park. Gradually he would be introduced to more of his kind and, with luck, might mate and produce a litter of cubs. A better way to provide a much needed breeding programme than the zoo could provide.

Just about everyone at the zoo was proud of the fact that they were acting on the public's new found interest and respect for animals held in captivity. The zoo was amongst the first to make such a change and it propelled their name to the forefront of the attention of a wider public. And that had boosted the zoo's income. How strange it now was that getting rid of the most popular animal could make the zoo more popular.

Of course, saying that just about everyone was proud meant that the feeling was not shared by everyone, not least by those keepers who had looked after the tiger with more care than if it had been their own domestic cat. There were two of them. An offer had been made to relocate one of them to another job within the zoo; but only one. The other would have to go. The question was who? And the question was debated by the management as well as the two staff. Would it be last in first out? Would it be the oldest or the youngest? If it was the oldest and longest serving the redundancy payment would be greater. So all eyes turned to the younger of the two.

Jack, the young keeper, desperately wanted to stay. He was willing to take on any other job as long as he could remain at the zoo. Eugene, the older, more unusually named keeper had been there from the time that the tiger had arrived. He had arrived with it. Apparently he had worked in Nepal and had been part of the team that had captured the animal. Because of the question of redundancy the personnel department had searched through the records of his employment to work out the costs. They had found the record of his first salary payment but had not found any paperwork relating to his application for employment. He had simply come with the tiger and automatically employed with it. It was not entirely surprising to personnel who knew that the filling of many of the jobs back then was due more to who you knew than what you knew. Although no-one was could deny that Eugene didn't have an in depth knowledge of the tiger. Which was a point made by the zoo's vet who often relied on Eugene for knowledge and help not just in treating the tiger but also in dealing with the ailments of many of the other animals, especially the larger ones.

The time had come for a decision. The tiger would be leaving in just over a week. The zoo's Director had to call in the two keepers and give them his decision. He arranged it for late on Friday afternoon. He would be away for the weekend at his cottage in Somerset, near Porlock on the edge Exmoor, and would be clear of any ill feelings if there were any.

Jack and Eugene both arrived in good time. They waited until nearly ten minutes after the appointed time before the secretary told them they could go in to the Director's office. Eugene was the one to knock. The Director called for them to enter and Eugene went in followed by Jack.

They stood in front of his large, dark wooden desk topped with an inlay of green leather. On it were a telephone, two old wooden file trays, and antique onyx pen and ink stand and a glass of water. In front of him were two buff folders. One folder looked considerably older than the other.

"Thank you for coming." Said the Director rather superfluously. "You are both, of course, well aware of the decision that has to be made. I only wish that the zoo had enough vacancies to keep you both in employment. Alas, that is not the case. And with the changes that are taking place in the modern zoo, the refocusing of our efforts on specific animals and the move away from the animals that need a greater amount of freedom and space than we can provide, openings are limited."

The Director took a breath and a sip of water.

"We have, of course, completed a full review of you employment, both of you,; what you have to offer the zoo and what the zoo is able to offer you, where you have strengths and where you have weaknesses. Not that there are many weaknesses I have to add. And both of you have served reliably and with dedication. There has never been a bad word written of either of you.

But a decision has to be made. And, regrettably, it is my duty to tell you what is."

He paused and shuffled the files.

"I'm sad to say, Eugene that it is you whom we have reluctantly decided to offer redundancy. You'll have a week's notice of course which will take you to the time when the tiger leaves for the wildlife park. I'm sure you will want to see him go."

He took out some paperwork from one of the files.

"This is the calculation for your redundancy payment. I'm sure you will find it quite generous. If you have any questions I'm sure personnel will be able to answer them."

The Director stood and held out his hand.

"Um," he said, "well, thank you for all your work here, Eugene."

Eugene looked at the hand. He sighed. He looked at the Director; looked into his eyes.

The Director moved his hand away. The man had always given him a strange feeling whenever he'd met him. His eyes had always had the look of the tiger's eyes. A different colour, but the feeling behind them could be almost the same.

"Yes, well, Jack, you'll be moving to the monkey enclosure. Report there on Monday morning."

The Director sat. It was the cue for Jack and Eugene to leave.

Neither had said a word. Jack was relieved but felt sorry for Eugene. Eugene seemed to have little care about what had happened. He had simply folded and pocketed the paperwork and calmly left the office to return to the tiger's cage. Jack had tried to speak to him, to say sorry for what had happened, but Eugene just walked on. They had never been close, it had been a workmanlike arrangement, but Eugene had taught Jack everything he could and Jack had appreciated it more than it might have appeared or than Eugene had, perhaps, realised.

Jack was not working that weekend, it was his one in four off, and as he'd come to the end of his shift he clocked off and went home.

Saturday and Sunday were the busiest days of the week at the zoo, especially when the weather was good or in the school holidays. This weekend though, it was not a holiday period and the weather was dark, cold and wet; visitor numbers were low. Even an hour before the official closing time the zoo was almost completely deserted and many of the enclosures were empty, their animal occupants having been moved into their warmer overnight quarters. A few people still wished to see the tiger but were disappointed. Because of the cold weather Eugene had opened the door to the warm indoor accommodation and had little trouble coaxing the animal in. The visitors left early a little disappointed. But at least, form the zoo's point of view, they didn't ask for any refunds. Not that they would have been successful, the weather could not be controlled, it was an act of God, and none would be forthcoming anyway.

The prompt closure that evening meant that the staff could get away earlier than usual. The only task that remained was for the security guards to thoroughly check the grounds and ensure that everyone, visitors and staff, had left and that all cages and enclosures were properly secured. They too finished their rounds quickly. All was well and in order and the guards could settle down in the warmth of their office only to take turns venturing out into the rain and cold to carry out checks throughout the night. Each time they did they signed off the paperwork to show that all was as it should be.

It wasn't until the zoo opened the next morning that something was found to be amiss.

Eugene had not reported for work. The immediate thought was that he had simply walked away from the job in anger at being made redundant. A call was made to jack's father to ask Jack to come in. Jack got there three quarters of an hour later.

Jack went to the admin block to pick up the keys for the tiger's cage; the door to the internal quarters was locked as it should be. But no keys for it hung in the key cupboard. And no-one had signed them out in the key register. In the Directors absence the head of security had to be called in to gain access to the safe which held the duplicate keys. Another hour went past.

The head of security arrived and opened the safe. He and one of his guards searched through the keys, several times. They could not find the duplicate. The head of security was not happy. Now a locksmith would have to be called in to open up the door. There was no chance of breaking through the door, it was a heavy metal one. Another hour went by before the locksmith arrived.

Jack was stationed at the external cage to explain to visitors that the tiger was unwell and so would not be coming out that day. They went away initially disappointed, but not unduly so, there was much else to see and they had been offered vouchers for a free elephant ride to keep them happy.

The locksmith arrived and got to work on the lock. It only took a few minutes to unpick, it was an old and quite simple lock. He stood aside as the head of security and jack walked passed and went inside.

They stood and looked at the tiger's quarters. Everything was secure, the barred doors would close and locked. All was in order, the straw bedding was fresh and clean, sufficient water was in the trough, and some meat still lay on the floor for the tiger to eat.

But there was no tiger.

-:-

The Director, Patrick Harding BSc, arrived at his cottage on the edge of Exmoor with his wife on Friday evening. The rain and clouds had begun to clear and there was a hint of red on the horizon which Patrick hoped would be a forecast of better weather the next day. The cottage was one of a rank that lined one side of a country lane a short distance from a village which still had a pub and a small shop. The row of cottages looked out across the road to a wooded hill beyond which were there were the forest and wide open gorse covered slopes that he and his wife liked to explore. On a good day they could see beyond Porlock to the blue waters of the Bristol Channel. Their second home and its location gave them everything they needed for a relaxed weekend away from the bustle of the city and work at the zoo.

His wife wished that they could spend every weekend there but that was impossible, Patrick had to spend at least every other week at his desk.

The next morning Patrick was blissfully unaware of the events about to unfold at the zoo. The weather was not as good as he had hoped. He had risen early leaving his wife in bed. She had, overnight, developed a chill and cold and had decided to lie in and try and shake it off. He was making breakfast for himself and a hot cup of tea for his wife at dawn. The breeze had stiffened bringing a patchwork of dark clouds scudding over the Bristol Channel and touching the tops of the moor. And these clouds of the morning sky were outlined in red; a shepherd's warning.

Patrick decided that, if the weather was to worsen later, he would take a walk into the woods and hills first thing and return for lunch. Any bad weather should hold off until then.

He bade his wife farewell, left the cottage, and took a track off the lane up the hill and into the woods. He had trekked the same way on many occasions and knew the path well. It was only just past 8am.

Hilary, Patrick's wife, had dozed in the warmth of her bed for several hours. She woke to the ringing of the telephone. It was an old fashioned black Bakelite model with a particularly loud bell. By the time she'd got out of bed and got to the phone downstairs on a small table by the front door, it has topped ringing.

She couldn't imagine it was anything important but it was time to get up anyway. She was feeling slightly better for having slept in, needed a hot drink, and prepare some lunch for Patrick's return; or perhaps they could go to the pub and save her having to make anything.

She ran herself a hot bath. Something else that should help soothe the cold. As luck would, or rather wouldn't, have it, as soon as she got into the bath the phone rang again. For a second she thought of getting out of the embrace of hot water and answering it, but only for a second. It surely couldn't be all that important; but whoever it was had phoned twice. She remained submerged and the phone fell silent.

By the time she'd finished her bath and was dressed it was 12.30. She expected Patrick's return within the next half hour or so.

The phone rang again. This time she got to it before the bell fell silent.

It was the zoo. The head of security was on the line and asking to speak to Patrick. She told him that he was out but should be back soon. She asked if there was any message she could give him. Only, the head of security had said, that he was to phone the zoo as soon as he returned.

For the next half hour or so Hilary busied herself about the cottage. By 13.15 she was ready for Patrick's return. She looked out of the front door and along the road then up into the hill to see if she could catch sight of him. The weather was getting worse. A south westerly wind was blowing more strongly and darker, lower clouds were descending upon the hills. The first spots of rain were staring to fall. She hoped Patrick would return very soon and not be caught in the deteriorating weather.

By 14.00 Patrick had not returned and the zoo had called again. Hilary was more worried. The rain had begun to fall hard in a gusting wind. And there was clearly something very urgent that the zoo needed him for.

They were both regular hill walkers and knew the procedures in case of a suspected emergency. Someone not returning at an appointed time in such weather could be treated as such. The local group of volunteers who came out to search for anyone were based at the pub. Hilary fist made a call to their number and left a message then walked to the pub to see if any of them were there. There was an outside chance, she thought, that Patrick may have gone there before coming home, although she doubted it, it would be very unlike him.

As soon as she arrived the volunteers had got the message. It was always better to start a search immediately and Hilary had done the right thing in alerting them early. There was probably nothing to worry about but it was better to get going straight away than wait. Preparations were quickly made and the volunteer group set off along the lane, first to check if Patrick had now returned, and then to take the same path into the hills to search for him.

He was not at the cottage. They would not let Hilary accompany them. She was told stay at the cottage near a phone or in case Patrick should return from a different route. Her neighbour had come by and said she would stay with Hilary until they got word.

The phone rang again.

Hilary told the head of security what was happening. He was silent for a moment and then told her that he would pass that news on. Before she had time to ask who he meant to pass it on to he had hung up.

The day dragged on. The afternoon went by and evening was about to fall. The weather had not improved. Patrick had not returned.

As darkness was finally came the volunteers returned. Patrick was not with them, they had not found him. They could do no more until the morning. But more volunteers including the police and men from a local army base would be brought in to continue the search.

When the phone rang again Hilary could not take the call, she was too upset and in tears.

Her neighbour passed on the news about Richard. She was told that the zoo's local constabulary would also be informed.

The next day dawned with clear blue skies and warm sunshine; a much better day for a search. Hilary had hardly slept. The neighbour had stayed with her throughout the night.

As three groups of searchers - volunteers, police and soldiers – were making ready for an early start there was a knock at the cottage door. Three police had come to see Hilary. Two were uniformed, one an Inspector the other a Policewoman, the third identified himself as a Detective Inspector from Bristol and was in plain clothes. They told her that the policewoman would remain with her until they had any news and that her neighbour could go home and get some rest herself. Another Constable would be stationed outside the cottage. To Hilary it seemed more than necessary.

It was the DI who began to ask Hilary questions about the zoo, Patrick's job, and what events from the previous week that Patrick may have discussed with her.

She was not sure why they were asking such questions, why would they want to know about his work? He never really discussed his work with her and hadn't said anything much recently.

But then she remembered the phone calls.

Something must have happened at the zoo. But whatever it was couldn't have anything to do with Patrick going missing on the moor.

The DI nodded, told her not to worry, it was all part of the routine, they had to ask all sort of questions, cover all angles, it was all part of the job. He thanked her, whispered something to the uniformed inspector, then they both left. The Policewoman suggested she made some tea; they may have some time to wait.

It was late that afternoon that Patrick's body was found, not by the searchers but by another hill walker. The police were very quickly on the scene. They immediately took charge, stood down the volunteers and sent the soldiers back to barracks. A helicopter was called and Patrick's body was flown from where it was found back to Bristol and a police car arrived to whisk Hilary back to her Bristol home.

The press hardly had time to get cameramen there before it was all over. The volunteers could tell the reporters very little other than what it was said the now anonymous hill walker had told one of them. And that story was the one that hit the headlines.

It was said the body had been badly mangled and bloodied. It was not found anywhere where Patrick could have fallen and sustained such injuries. Something else must have happened. The body looked as if he had been attacked by a savage beast.

Such a graphic story can remain in the headlines as long as no other story comes along to dislodge it and the minds of both the press and public quickly move on.

Within a matter of hours of the story becoming news there was a sinking of a passenger ferry in the Channel, a huge earthquake in California, a Government Minister resigning in disgrace, and the favourites to win the FA Cup being defeated by a non- league team.

Patrick's story was forgotten.

Almost forgotten.

For many years afterwards came the odd story of the sighting of a great beast, a cat it was said. Blurred photographs sometimes emerged. Farmers sheep were suddenly mauled or slaughtered by some vicious animal which all shepherds insisted could not be a dog or a fox. Time and again the story of a giant cat like beast was told on a dark night around the warmth of a pub fire.

The zoo's tiger was never found. But as far as the public and most of the zoo's employees were concerned they were told the same as was given in the newspaper report; it was said that it had died from a mixture of the cold weather and an unknown virus.

Eugene; Eugenius Guy to give him his full name, was never traced. He was never seen again.

Well, only very rarely, and only by the unfortunate few.

Zig-Zag Street

Many would not know that it was a street. They would pass it each day without a thought, almost without recognition of its existence. To them it was just an obscure gap between two buildings into which only a narrow wedge of light would ever encroach.

Into it a few people would venture. Those who would use it most would only go as far as the sunlight reached and these were the people whose lives were lived upon the streets, who could claim a few meters of ground against the walls on one side or the other as their home for the night.

The street was not a street even if called so. It was no more that a narrow lane. Beyond the point taken by the homeless it changed from a flat surface into a series of steps. They turned one way and then the other rising up a hillside. On either side were the walls of buildings but very few windows and only one or two doors. The windows were heavily curtained or blinded and the doors were old and grimy and looked as though they had never opened since they were constructed.

In daylight, even though shrouded in shadow, there were some people who would use it as a short cut. If you knew of its existence, where it led and were willing to trudge up the countless steps it could save you a long detour to get to the main road at the top.

Ryan knew of it, and used it. He worked at an office not far from the top. It was quite a climb. He would often have to stop half way to catch his breath telling himself it was good for him and kept him fit. He had never counted the total number of steps but had sometimes thought of doing so. Once or twice he had started to count but had given up. And so the steps remained countless.

He would normally use it during daylight hours either going up to work on the mornings or, less tiring, coming back down again at the end of the working day. He could not recall ever having met anyone on his climb or descent.

He avoided it when dark. That meant he rarely used it in the winter when it was dark at the start of the working day as well as at the end. Not because of the stories that were told about it but because it was unlit and the steps would be wet, slipper, icy and dangerous. At least, that was his excuse.

But there was a day when his usual bus into the city didn't turn up and, although he always gave himself enough time, sometimes enough to stop for an early morning coffee between the bus stop and his office, catching the following bus would probably make him late.

When he got off the bus he only had five minutes to get to the office. It was mid-winter with thick clouds low in the sky, cold and still dark. He came to the opening to Zig-Zag Street. He looked at his watch. It was 8.25 and he was due to be at the office at 8.30. To take the detour he would be late. He decided he would take the steps up Zig-Zag Street.

He edged passed a couple of rough sleepers and in to the dark shadows of the street and began his climb up the steps. It was very dark, wet and slippery. He didn't rush; he took it carefully but kept going as fast as he could. The steps turned left and right. At each turn it flattened out. At what he recognised as the half way point he stopped to take a breath then started again.

The steps seemed to go on forever. He couldn't remember it being this far before.

He came to a turn and a flatter piece of ground. He stopped. It was odd but it looked to him as if it was the halfway point again. He looked at his watch; 8.25. His watch must have stopped; it had to be at least five minutes later than that. He should be near the top of the street, the main road, and his office. He took out his phone to check the time. It was the same; 8.25.

He was sure it couldn't be. He was going to be late. He found his office number on his phone and selected it to tell them he was going to be late. Nothing; there was no signal. The high walls of the buildings each side must be blocking the signal. He tried one more time; still no signal.

He must hurry. He must be near the top.

He went more quickly, now and then taking two steps at a time.

He was breathing hard and stopped.

He was at a turn. He looked around. It was the same turn. Again he was only half way up. He shook his head. This was impossible. He told himself to keep calm, control himself. What if he went back down the steps, back down to the main road? He would then take the detour. He would be even later, but what did that matter now?

He set off down the steps, turning left, turning right.

Breathing hard, he stopped.

This could not be possible. It could not be happening. Once more he was at the half way point. Whether he went up or if he went down he was there again.

He stopped and leant against a wall. He got his breathing under control. He had to think. It reminded him of something. He had seen something like this before. It was a drawing, a three dimensional one. Steps going up and steps going down but whichever way you went, either up or down, you just kept going, you always ended up where you started. But that was a drawing, a two dimensional drawing pretending to be three dimensional. It could not work actually work in three dimensional life. He knew it couldn't, he had read about it. It could only happen as a drawing on a piece of paper. They were the endless stairs, the Penrose stairs he surprisingly remembered they were called.

But here he was, halfway up and halfway down.

Again he looked at his watch and then his phone. It was 8.25.

That was something else that couldn't happen.

He calmed himself. He would go down one more time, slowly, taking his time, making sure that each turn he took was not a false one. Perhaps there was one that was a side turning that he had not seen before, that he had inadvertently taken.

Down he went, steadily, a step at a time. He counted them, just as he had begun to do previously, as he had always intended to do. Four turns, two left and two right, and eighty steps later he stopped at the half way point. He had got nowhere. He looked at his watch. It was 8.25. He took out his phone; still no signal and still 8.25.

Close by the half way point there was an old wooden door. He had passed it and not noticed it before. This time he did. This time he noticed it because there was a small line of light coming from a narrow gap underneath it, between it and the street.

There would be someone in the building, someone behind the door, someone who could help him.

He went to the door, hesitated for a moment, then knocked; lightly at first and then another louder knock.

He waited.

He heard a noise behind the door. He knocked once more. He saw the slit of light at the bottom of the door dim with a shadow. Someone was behind the door. He heard the sound of a lock or latch grating as it was turned.

He almost felt the tug the door was given as the person tried to open it. It was stiff, it was almost completely sealed, unused for many years.

Suddenly it broke open and a yellow shaft of light spilled out into Zig-Zag Street. Silhouetted in front of it was the figure of a man.

"Please." Pleaded Ryan. "I need to get down to the main road. I can't seem to get there. Or the road above."

"This door has not been open for many a year." Said the silhouette.

"Uh, no, I could see that, it was very stiff. If you let me in could you let me out into the main road? Or anywhere other than this street."

"Anywhere? Other than this street?"

"Please, I just need to get away from it, it's not going anywhere."

"The street does not lead anywhere. But anywhere is where you want to go?"

"Yes, anywhere, anywhere but here."

"Are you sure you wish for that?"

Ryan felt a chill and a shiver go through him at the sound of the man's voice. "Yes," he said, "I just want to get away from here."

"Very well." Said the man as he stepped forward.

Ryan could now make out his face. He had piercing blue-black eyes and, although not smiling, showed his teeth, one of which was pure gold. His hair was black and grew in waves and curls. His clothes were old and heavy.

"You are right." Said the man. "This is no place for you. Anywhere else is better than this. I will take you there."

Ryan saw the man's hand move. It went to his coat pocket. In a flash it was out again and with an actual flash Ryan saw the steel of a blade.

He had no time to move. The man was fast. The arm and with it the knife struck quickly. A six inch blade thrust forward into Ryan's chest, or rather just below it. And as six inches of it had entered Ryan's chest it struck upward into his heart.

Ryan saw it in slow motion, felt it as a slow searing pain, and gave in to it in a slow slump to the ground.

The door closed and the small strip of light was extinguished as Ryan lay in a growing pool of blood.

The clouds were breaking and the sun was rising. It was 8.30. Sunlight began to fill the space between the buildings that was Zig-Zag Street and in its light the first of the daylight's commuters decided to take the shortcut to the main road above.

At 8.35 the police received a call. A body had been found in Zig-Zag Street.

Despite weeks of effort and enquiries the police still had no idea who had killed Ryan Jeffries. No weapon had ever been found and nothing seemed to have been taken from his pockets.

The rough sleepers had seen and heard nothing. But they never did. These were the people who had no homes; they had nowhere to go. But, of course, if they wished, they could have gone anywhere.

Random Acts

Guy Savage had worked at various jobs throughout his life. He had done many things. He had done enough to retire early. A business he had set up and managed for seven years had grown quickly. From small beginnings he had expanded to cover all the main urban areas of the country, and he had done so without having to borrow from the banks, it had all been self financing. What the company was worth at the end of those seven years he was worth.

But the market had changed. He had seen that new competitors and changes in technology along with people's habits meant that profits would begin to be squeezed and, perhaps in a few years, the market might even collapse leaving the company worth almost nothing. So he decided to sell up.

He was lucky, others had not looked so deeply and carefully into the future and were still keen to enter the marketplace and make what they thought would be easy money. After a series of quite short negotiations he agreed to sell the company to a merchant bank who were also buying some of his smaller competitors in the hope of controlling the entire market. Once they had completed the due diligence he pocketed the money.

Now he was very comfortably off, lived in a substantial property and had time on his hands.

That, in a way, was becoming a problem. The first few weeks and even months were a pleasure. He could rest, read, go where and when he wanted, and all without any interruptions; no urgent phone calls, last minute meetings or problems to sort out. I those now managing the business could cope why couldn't they when he was in charge. That one was easy to answer. Whoever made the decisions would take the flak if things went wrong. In the past the buck had stopped with him, his managers would be safe from criticism, they had him as their shield.

But now, after six months, and when the winter weather was drawing in, he was feeling bored. The garden was in hibernation and even the large conservatory would feel cold unless strong sunlight streamed through.

He could have travelled. Gone to the sunshine, go wherever he wanted to go. But he was on his own, he'd never married, and for now he had travelled and seen all he wanted to during the summer. And increasing boredom brought on a sort of laziness. They more he decided not to do something the less likely he was to want to do anything. Except for perhaps one thing, he never tired of reading. He still devoured a large number of books. He had a substantial bookcase that covered an entire wall of what he called his library.

Anyone looking at his collection of books would see that, although he read a variety of novels from science fiction, fantasy and historical works mostly of the Roman Empire, by far the majority of them on the shelves were murder mysteries. There were a large number by well known American and British authors both modern and from the past as well as more obscure works.

One day as he moped about the house with the lights still on in the daytime whilst outside heavy black clouds released a curtain of cold steady rain and sleet, and as he ran a finger over the spines of the books, that he began to think.

Every book he had read had ended with the uncloaking of the killer. He could not remember any where the police, or more likely than not an amateur sleuth, had failed to get their man, or woman, either alive or more rarely dead.

Even reading newspaper reports of such crimes it seemed that the police found the killers. Or did they? Perhaps the murders they were unable to solve merely, in the end, got shelved and the news of them faded from the papers and the interest in them faded from the public's mind.

He decided it would be interesting to find out. He left the library and went to a small office attached to it where he had a computer with two screens on a large mahogany table with an orthopaedic chair.

He began a search of all murders and reported in the press over the previous five years and then tried to trace the stories though to their logical end of the perpetrators conviction. That proved very difficult. After initial reports the press often tired of the news and the thread he wanted to follow was broken.

So he changed tack. He searched the official statistics. He should have started that way, it was much easier. At least, he felt, those of the UK could be accepted as pretty reliable.

The police's own statistics showed that they had a clear up rate of 95%, just about the highest in the world. But it still left 5% not solved. He found the latest figures. 574 people were murdered in the previous year. That was considerably more than he had imagined from looking at newspaper reports; they obviously only concentrated on those that were of interest to them at any particular time; when other news was at a low ebb. It meant that 29 murders during the previous year alone were not solved. And 29 murders were still at large. Or that a single serial killer had committed 29 murders and had not been caught. And it would mean that, maybe, over the past five years 145 people had been murdered and the police had never found the perpetrators. It was not like the stories in the crime novels.

Why had these people been killed? Who had killed them? Most murders are between people who know each other, more often than not family members. The police would always start their investigations on that premise. Even if that were not the case there was bound to be a motive. It was discovering that motive that was the key to unlocking a case. Even if the motive was known the killer must have the opportunity and the means to carry out the deed. And then there was the forensic evidence. In the old days it may have been nothing more than a fingerprint or a discarded cigarette butt or a footprint. It was still those obvious things, but now there was much more detailed forensic evidence. The tiniest trace of DNA could link a suspect to the crime scene as well as the smallest of other samples. It seemed almost impossible not to leave some sort of trace behind, to be so careful that, even in the act and inevitable struggle of killing a human being, no trace of the murderer could be left.

At lunch time he left his office, had some lunch and mulled over what he had found out. Why had those people been killed? Why had the cases never been solved? What if that one and most important reasons for murder, motive, was not necessarily involved? In most of those unsolved cases there probably was a motive even if the police had not figured it out. But what if in some cases there was none, none other than the act of the murder itself. A carefully planned and executed act for the simple pleasure of the killing, nothing other than the pure sadistic satisfaction and thrill of it. The act of a psychopath perhaps, the act of someone with no remorse for what they do. Maybe someone would do it purely to prove it could be done and done without being caught.

There were books about such people but, contrary to them getting away with it, they had been caught.

He went back to the books on his shelves, He had some books which told such stories, true crimes, real life murders. But why had these people been caught? He spent the rest of the day and evening scanning though them. And the next day too.

By lunchtime he had come to a decision. He believed he knew why some were caught and others not. He believed he knew the answer as soon a she had begun checking the stories, and now he was sure.

Even those psychopaths who had been caught had fitted the mould. Far from not having a motive they had one, it was the fulfilment of their lust to kill; that was motive enough for them. All they needed was the opportunity and the means. For those they just needed time and planning. And if they were in no particular hurry it need not be rushed. Unfortunately for the failures they allowed the emotions that controlled their lust take over. They did not take the necessary time for the most careful preparations needed for a successful operation and so made their mistakes, mistakes the police could detect.

Their one big failing was usually creating a pattern. Because of their emotional needs, no matter how logically they approached their crime they left a pattern behind. They needed not have calculated things so meticulously but to allow a randomness to direct their crime and randomness to the act that left no pattern for the police to detect.

Perhaps that was the modus operandi of those who were never caught. Their act was a random one.

The more he thought about it the more it intrigued him. How possible would it be? How would one go about setting up such a scenario?

First of all, motive. That was awkward, because of course there was one. It was purely theoretical of course, but the motive was simply to find out if it was possible to plan and carry out a completely random and undetectable murder. But at least there would be no emotion involved in it. It was, he had told himself, purely theoretical and so the most unlikely motive to be considered as one.

Next, opportunity. That, he believed, would be dependent upon time and place. And that was where the randomness could be introduced. Pick somewhere, anywhere in the UK – although not choosing anywhere in the world would dilute the randomness – and then a time.

Finally, the means. A weapon of some sort would have to be used, and it must be untraceable, or something so common and easily obtained that it would not be possible to trace.

He had a large map of the UK. He took it to the garage and hung it on the wall. He dug out from a box an old set of darts. He pulled a bobble hat over his eyes, turned around twice, was sure he still faced the map, and threw a dart. He'd always been useless at darts as he had no idea where it might land. He pulled back the hat. The dart was sticking out of the wall and had pierced the map. He went over and bent down to look at it. It had landed on the city of Bristol.

How tempting it would be to carry out his own crime. He had taken these steps, it would not take much more to carry on, to see it through. But did he have the backbone to do so audacious and unfeeling and evil an act.

He was not sure that such a thing was not in his character, not part of his psyche. Did he have the guts and the nerve for such an unwarranted, unnecessary and deliberate act of malevolence? But did he believe he could do it? Now that he better understood such a crime, was it possible? Would he be able to commit one of those murders that the police had given up on, one of those that had all the hallmarks of a completely random killing, one with no meaning or motive, a senseless death. And could he get away with it?

He need not actually go so far as to commit the crime, but he could see if it could be done. He could test out the theory. He need not strike the fatal blow. It was, he told himself, an exercise to see if it was possible.

The dart had shown him the way.

He had picked a place at random. Once there he could pick a time as randomly as possible. But it could not be entirely so. It could not be random in so far as he had to find somewhere that was not busy, that was at least partly hidden from public view, that few people used, but that at least one random person would use. He looked for a suitable location. An old newspaper report had caught his eye. There had been a murder in a dark deserted street. It had a bad reputation and was avoided by most people after dark. He would take a look at it. This might be a suitable scene for his crime even if it had been used by someone before. In fact, that made it all the more intriguing to him. He would be creating a pattern that was not a pattern, it was a coincidence, and the police might look for something that was not there. In fact, the addition of his crime might goad the police into investigating the old one and, if they made progress and caught a suspect, he would be the one to be blamed for both. A more perfect crime than he had intended.

Guy Savage made his mind up. He would go to Bristol. He must not leave a trail. He must use cash and that cash must not be seen to be coming from his account outside of a fairly normal pattern of withdrawals. For two weeks he regularly withdrew cash from his usual bank, but rather more than he would normally take. He spent almost none of it and saved the rest.

But there was also the question of what weapon to use, something that could not be traced. He had something in the garage. It was old, he had been given it as a child by his grandfather. It was a hunting knife. There was no chance, even if found by some unlikely coincidence, that it could be traced to him. An old blade that he could sharpen with an old wooden handle that would have been made a century ago and the existence of which was known by no one but himself. He chose this weapon.

He would not drive to Bristol, he would take the train, and he would buy the ticket in cash at the railway station. He would not be using any of his cards whilst he was away from home.

He arrived in the late afternoon and booked into a cheap bed and breakfast some distance from the street in question. Luckily the owner was quite brusque and had not asked him what he was doing in town. After unpacking he took a bus to the area, again making sure he used cash, and took a stroll around the area close to Zig-Zag Street, the crime scene. Nearby there was a pub. A pub was a great place for new and gossip. Information was given freely – well, for the cost of a couple of pints.

After the first drink Guy mentioned that he had to get to an address which was at the top of the hill. He asked the barman the best way to get there. There was one thing the barman was most sure of, and that was not to take the short cut up Zig-Zag Street, especially after dark. It was a dangerous place. Only a year ago someone had been found murdered there. It was best to go the long way around.

After another drink Guy left the pub and casually walked past the turning to the street. It was dark now and two rough sleepers had already made their beds for the night where the street lights kept the blackness of the Zig-Zag Street at bay.

He headed back to the bed and breakfast. He had to admit that he didn't fancy investigating the street at night, at least not yet. He would have his first look at the intended crime scene in daylight.

Guy had made sure to bring and wear the most well-used and non-descript clothes he could find. He made sure he had a coat with a hood which could have been bought in any of the larger shops, and he had spent time in his garage working on the trainers he was wearing to eliminate their treat. He looked as ordinary person as he could be, and everything would be destroyed afterwards.

He walked the area close to the street but staying clear of it. He did not loiter and after one pass did not return again for at least half an hour. What he was looking for were any security or traffic cameras. He needed to know where they were and if they were directed at the street's entrance.

During the half hour intervals he took the long way around to the top of the street and its other entrance/exit. Again he checked for any security cameras.

It took him several sorties but he was sure that there were none that covered the comings and goings of the street. A fact that had not helped the police during the previous murder investigation and one that had not been rectified.

In the afternoon he was on the main road at the top of the hill. He would take his first look at Zig-Zag Street.

He took the steps down it. He went right and left. At each turn the path flattened. High walls rose either side of it, the walls of buildings and, he believed, some of hidden gardens. There were few doors or windows in them. What windows there were, were high up, what few doors there were, were old and looked as if they were unused, unopened for many years. It was dark between those walls even in the afternoon sunlight.

He reached the bottom. It straightened out and led to the main road he had walked earlier. At the entrance there was the detritus of the rough sleepers.

He knew it would be easier going down rather than up. And he did not want to be seen by the homeless people at the bottom. He decided to use the upper entrance.

He had seen no-one else in the street when he came down so wanted to keep it under surveillance to find out how often it was used. He'd seen a cafe at the top on the other side of the main road. He would go the long way around and watch it for a while from there.

He stayed as long as he could, reading his paper and doing the crossword, without overstaying. In that time he saw two people going down and just one person coming out of the street.

The afternoon light was waning, it would soon be getting dark. Darkness was the ally to the crime he had committed to. Should he follow someone down the street? No, it would be too obvious. If he entered on his own, in no way related to another person, that would be best. He could wait halfway down, in the shadows. He could take his time. Someone, randomly, would either come up or down the steps of the street. All he needed to do was wait for his victim.

He left the cafe and wandered along the main road. The street lights came on as darkness fell. He crossed the road and headed back to Zig-Zag Street. He raised the hood of his coat both to hide his appearance and against the fine rain that was beginning to fall. Without pausing he turned into the street and descended the steps.

It was dark, darker than he had expected. The walls loomed menacingly over him. It was wet and the steps were slippery. He took his time and descended them with care especially as he had no grip on the soles of his trainers.

He reached the mid way point. A short flight of steps had taken him straight down after a turn to the left. There was a flat piece of ground before it turned to the right. The corner of the turn on the flat ground was so much in shadow and so dark that he could almost disappear within it.

He pulled his jacket close and his hood as far as it would go. He kept his hands in his pockets. In one of them was the hunting knife.

He waited, the fine rain settling on him.

He heard footsteps. It was difficult to tell whether they came from above or below as they echoed between the high walls.

He stayed still, his back against the wall, hugging the darkness.

The black shape of a figure cam through the gloom from the steps below its outline only just discernible against it. It came to a stop only a few yards from him. He held his breath. Without thinking he had clutched the hilt of the hunting knife in his pocket.

The figure stopped, not by the wall, but by the outline of a door that Guy had only just noticed. It was one of those so barely used that its shape had almost fused with the wall.

There was movement from the figure and a sound. It was the jangling of keys. Guys saw the person's hand reach out to the door and then heard the grating of an old lock turning. As it turned a thin line of light appeared around the edge of the door. It opened. Dull orange light flooded out into the street.

The figure, which Guy now realised was a man, was framed in the oblong of the doorway light. The man turned back to face the street as he was about to close the door behind him.

It was then he saw Guy, no longer in shadow, now lit by then orange light.

Without thinking Guy had pulled his knife from its sheath.

The man growled. Guy could see his face; sharp piercing eyes looked out from under black wavy hair. His growl turned to a snarl that exposed his teeth. They were remarkably white, all but one which was a sparkling gold.

The man came forward. He was surprisingly fast. But in his moment of fear, so was Guy. As Guy saw the flash of metal in the man's hand his own hand came out of his pocket with the blade of his knife facing forward.

The man rushed without thinking and taking care. In a few strides he would be on top of Guy. But the stone surface was wet and slippery. On is final step he slipped. His eyes widened. He gasped. He fell forward almost in slow motion. His arms reached out to steady himself. Guy's hand still held his knife and the blade still faced forward. As the man fell his own knife arm moved away from Guy. His knife hit the wall to Guy's side. Was wrenched from the man's grasp and fell with a sharp clang to the ground. At the same time the man fell further forward. He fell onto Guy's knife. It struck him and entered his body as his face was only inches away from Guy's. Surprise, consternation, disbelief and finally pain filled the man's eyes and face. He slid down. As he slid Guy's knife thrust upward and even deeper into him, into his heart.

Guy heard the man say something. Just a few words as he slipped to the ground.

"No. Not now. Not here. It cannot be."

And then he was at Guy's feet. Guy heard a final breath leave the man's body. He looked at his knife. It had come away from the body as it finished its fall. He looked at the blade and the blood upon it. And he looked at the blood upon his hand.

He could not believe what had happened. But was it not what he had planned, what he had wished for?

He brought himself quickly to his senses. He must go, leave this place. He would go up not down, not to where the rough sleepers might be.

He was about to move, to run up the steps when he heard the sound of someone approaching. Was it from above or below? Again because of the echo he could not tell. But he must get away.

The door was still open, the light still spilling from it onto the wet stones, some now covered in blood.

He ran to the door. It was the only way he could go, the only way to safety. The keys were still in the door. He took them. He went in and closed the door as quietly as he could, locked it, and leaned against it breathing heavily.

He was in a room empty of any furnishings. It was lit by old fashioned lamps, gas lamps Guy thought. On each of the other three walls there was a door. Three doors each one of which could lead him to safety. At least he hoped so. He looked at the bunch of keys. There were four of them, one for each door he presumed.

He would have to choose one.

He must choose a door for his escape, a door that could take him away from this place, take him to safety; take him anywhere other than here.

-:-

Another murder in Zig-Zag Street. The police would be under pressure to find the killer. The press talked of a serial killer. No-one would use the street until security was improved. Street lights need to be erected. Cameras must be installed. And the perpetrator must be found.

But as usual other headlines take over the front pages and the murder fades into history.

For the police this latest murder was even more frustrating. Not only could they, once again, find no clues whatsoever, but they could not identify the deceased. There was nothing on him that told of who he was. His picture produced no results from any other force. No-one had recognised him, no-one had ever seen him. In an age where we all leave some trace of ourselves it was most unusual.

-:-

Another force had another mystery. A man's disappearance. There was nothing to suggest why or where he had gone. His cards were never used again. There was no trace of him in the real world or in the ethereal, the vast banks of data that track our lives. It was most unusual in this day and age.

Stories
Of
Lost
Souls

Any resemblance to any person living or dead or to any location mentioned in the text of any story is purely coincidental.

Copyright: Peter F Damsberg

Printed in Great Britain
by Amazon